FOCUS ON THE FAMILY®

Christian Heritage Series

THE CHARLESTON YEARS

W9-AVC-067

The Misfit

Nancy Rue

BETHANY HOUSE PUBLISHERS
MINNEAPOLIS, MINNESOTA 55438

A Focus on the Family book published by
Bethany House Publishers
A Ministry of Bethany Fellowship International
11400 Hampshire Avenue South
Minneapolis, Minnesota 55438
www.bethanyhouse.com

Printed in the United States of America by
Bethany Press International, Minneapolis, Minnesota 55438

Library of Congress Cataloging-in-Publication Data

Rue, Nancy N.
    The misfit / Nancy Rue.
        p. cm. — (Christian Heritage series ; 13)
    Summary: Living with his uncle on a South Carolina plantation in 1860, eleven-year-old Austin befriends a young slave boy and learns more about how Jesus loves people who are different.
    ISBN 1-56179-560-7
    [1. Slavery—Fiction. 2. Afro-Americans—Fiction. 3. South Carolina—Fiction. 4. Christian life—Fiction.] I. Title. II. Series: Rue, Nancy N. Christian heritage series ; the Charleston years; bk. 13.
PZ7.R88515Mi   1997
[Fic]—dc21   97–24445
                                                                            CIP
                                                                             AC

98   99   00   01   02   03   04   05   /   12   11   10   9   8   7   6   5   4   3   2

For Mairin and Chamaea Tausch,
who are not afraid to be unique.

Canaan Grove Plantation,
Charleston
1860-1861

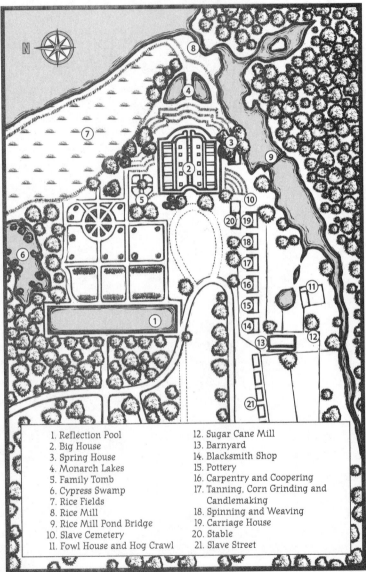

1. Reflection Pool
2. Big House
3. Spring House
4. Monarch Lakes
5. Family Tomb
6. Cypress Swamp
7. Rice Fields
8. Rice Mill
9. Rice Mill Pond Bridge
10. Slave Cemetery
11. Fowl House and Hog Crawl
12. Sugar Cane Mill
13. Barnyard
14. Blacksmith Shop
15. Pottery
16. Carpentry and Coopering
17. Tanning, Corn Grinding and Candlemaking
18. Spinning and Weaving
19. Carriage House
20. Stable
21. Slave Street

As soon as Austin Hutchinson's golden-brown eyes opened, the questions started popping into his head, and, of course, he asked them. That was just the way it was with him. He pressed his forehead, fringed with deer-colored hair, against the train window, licked the train soot from his lips, and started asking.

"Why are those black children—the ones running beside the train—why are they wearing only those shirts down to their knees? Don't they have pants on? Aren't they cold?"

He felt the window, early morning chilly against his face, and continued on. "I know it's South Carolina—but it's January! Oh, there are those buildings again. Are those the necessaries? I read that some of them have as many as *eight* toilets in them! Now *that* one, that must be a plantation house! It looks like a Greek temple—like I've seen in the books. Those columns are Ionic, aren't they? Or are they Corinthian?"

Across from him, his father, Wesley Hutchinson, blinked

1

open his bleary, gray-blue eyes and looked at the window. He'd been dozing on the hard-backed wooden seat, sitting straight up with Mother's doe-colored head in his lap where she slept, pale and sickly under her blankets.

Father was still half asleep, Austin could tell, but he knew he would answer his questions. He always did. Austin had spent most of his 11 years on trains—and in carriages and stagecoaches and inns. There wasn't much else to do *but* ask questions.

"I've heard that's the way they dress the slave children," Father said. "No trousers until they're 13."

"Slave children," Austin said. "Then we're getting close to Charleston."

He gathered his long, thin, lanky legs under him and got up on his knees to get a clearer look outside. Beside him, his six-year-old brother, Jefferson, whined in his sleep and curled himself into a chubby ball.

"I wear trousers," he mumbled sleepily.

"Please don't wake him up," Austin's mother murmured in her soft, lilting voice. "We just got him back to sleep."

No danger of me *waking him up,* Austin thought. *I like him best when he's asleep.*

Austin spotted another house at the end of an avenue lined with huge oak trees.

"That one had Corinthian columns," he pointed out. "Was that a plantation?"

Austin's father carefully shifted Mother's head. "That was one of the lesser plantation houses," he said. "Wait until you see Canaan Grove. I understand it's quite outlandish."

Austin didn't miss the edge in his father's tone. Although Wesley Hutchinson looked like a gentle man—lean and tall like Austin was getting to be, but with large, liquid eyes and soft, dark hair like Jefferson's—he was capable of hating. When Austin saw that curled-up look on his face and heard that tight sound in his voice, he knew he was doing it.

"If you hate the plantation owners so much," Austin said, "does that mean you hate Uncle Drayton, too?"

"I don't hate *them*," Father said. "I hate the fact that they own slaves—and I hate the fact that I am taking my family straight into slave-owning territory."

"Now, you *know* why we're going," Sally Hutchinson said patiently. "I simply can't travel with you until I'm stronger, and the boys and I need to be with family."

"I know," Father grumbled. "And your brother is the only family we have left." He writhed in his seat. "But I'll still fear for the three of you when I've returned to the North."

Ever since Austin could remember, his parents had been abolitionists. Those were the people who didn't believe it was right for one human being to own another, the way the southern planters did when they bought Negro slaves and made them work on their cotton and rice plantations.

Austin's mother and father had devoted their whole lives to writing pamphlets and newspaper articles and traveling around giving speeches about the evils of slavery. They would endure anything to convince people that slavery was against God's will.

"It can't be any more dangerous than some of the things we've already been through," Mother said.

"That's right," Austin said matter-of-factly. "You remember when that mob threw eggs in your face when you were lecturing?"

Father nodded.

"And when they set the building on fire where we were

staying? Mother almost died there from the smoke!"

"We *remember,* Austin," Sally Hutchinson said, using her it's-time-for-you-to-hush-up tone.

Austin craned his neck to see out the window again, where palm trees waved and palmettos stretched out their pointy leaves like surprised fans.

"It looks so different from up North," he said.

"I grew up here on this very land," Mother said. She lifted her head, too, to get a glimpse. "I told you, it's going to be *very* different."

Austin squirmed excitedly. "I'll be able to ride horses, you said. I've never even been on one. I wonder if they have thoroughbreds or just dobbins—I've read about both. And I can go hunting. I know everything from a Colt revolver to a Springfield rifle from pictures, but I've never even held a gun in my hand!"

"Neither have I," his father said, his voice pointed. "I've never seen the need to."

I'd better *hush up,* Austin thought.

But it was all he could do to hide how anxious he was to be at Canaan Grove. The thought of staying in one place, a place so new and filled with possible man-type adventures he didn't have to just read about in books—that thought shoved everything else into the background. Even the evils of slavery.

The clacking sounds of the Southern Line cars suddenly began to come farther and farther apart beneath them as the train slowed, and Austin knew they were coming to the out-skirts of Charleston. He pushed his face harder against the window.

Three children bundled up in ragged coats and cockeyed caps were walking along the road that paralleled the tracks.

They were holding hands as they huddled together, puffing damp morning air out of their mouths and talking away.

As he watched them grow smaller in the distance, Austin felt something move inside him. *They're friends with each other,* he thought.

Friends. He'd never really had any, not with always being on the move with his parents. And that was the thing that excited him the most about going to Canaan Grove. He had cousins there, three of them—Kady, 16, Polly, 13, and Charlotte, 11, his age. They were all girls, but that was all right. At least they were other children besides fit-pitching Jefferson, and they were going to be the first real friends he'd ever had.

He'd spent his whole life reading books about people— friends—having adventures together. Now at Canaan Grove he could have them. It made Austin feel as if he couldn't wait another second to be there.

"Will we get to Uncle Drayton's by carriage or by boat?" he asked. "I wonder, does he have a packet boat? They can sail mighty fast—"

Jefferson Hutchinson popped his dark head up from the seat with his round eyes already shimmering with anticipation.

"What carriage?" he said. "What boat?"

"Never you mind, shrimp," Austin said. "I'm asking the questions."

"You always ask them. It's my turn!" Jefferson's grin with its tiny teeth shrank into a warning pout.

Austin could feel his own face darkening. Jefferson was gearing up for what his mother called a "hissy fit," during which anything could occur, from getting kicked by a flying foot to seeing your knapsack go sailing across the room. The best thing, Austin knew, was to bite his tongue and ask later. But he was tired of always waiting on his bratty brother.

"It's my question," Austin said stubbornly.

"All right, then," Jefferson said. "I'll ask someone else."

Jefferson bolted from the seat and took off down the aisle, bumping elbows and stepping on skirt ruffles as he charged through.

"Jefferson, come back here!" Father hissed.

But Jefferson disappeared under the seat of a well-dressed couple who were dozing behind their newspaper.

Mother struggled up onto one elbow and looked down the aisle. "Oh, no, Wesley, he's going to disturb someone!"

"He's already put his footprint on that lady's parasol," Austin said.

"Go and fetch him back here, Austin," Father said.

With a weighty sigh, Austin loped down the aisle. Passengers were already peering curiously under their seats and clasping their handbags to their chests as the woman screeched, "There's something under my skirt!"

"Excuse me," Austin said. "I think it's my brother."

The woman continued squalling. Her husband lifted the edge of his wife's skirt, and from under the flounce of lace, a chubby six-year-old hand could be plainly seen.

Austin lunged down and grabbed it, yanking the rest of Jefferson out with it and shoving him on his belly toward the back of the car. The din of male laughter and female tongue clicking echoed in Austin's ears as he picked up Jefferson by the back of his pants and deposited him roughly on the seat.

"Where on earth was he?" Father said.

Austin glanced at his mother. Now that more light was filtering in from the morning sky, he could see that her face was pale and pinched. As she waited for Austin to answer, she began to cough, a gravelly sound that came all the way from the pit of her chest.

Austin just shrugged. "He was up there."

"We'll be pulling into the station any minute," Father said. "Let's get our things together."

As Austin got down on his knees to reach his mother's leather-handled satchel, there was a chorus of cries from the passengers farther up in the car.

"What is it now?" Wesley Hutchinson said impatiently.

"It can't be Jefferson this time," Mother said.

Austin jerked up as a figure in a black uniform shot past them, shouting, "Where is he?"

"Here!" a gentleman in a black top hat cried. He was standing up on the seat, pointing to a small door that was fixed into the train like a closet.

"What's happening, Wesley?" Sally Hutchinson said.

"I don't know, but I don't like the sound of it."

The "sound of it" was a low growl that seemed to go through the crowd around the closet door as if a bear were in their midst. It was the same sound made by the mob that had attacked Austin's father.

"I want to see!" Jefferson said, tugging on Austin's pant leg. "Lift me up! I want to *see!*"

Austin hoisted Jefferson up onto his narrow shoulders. The conductor flung open the closet door, and the crowd gasped together.

"Father, look at that!" Jefferson squealed. "There's a black man hiding in the closet!"

✝ ⋅✝⋅ ✝

Chapter Two

"**S**weet mother of Francis Marion, it's a runaway!" a man shouted.

The whole crowd closed in on the closet with shrieks erupting from them like thrusting spears.

"Runaway slave!"

"Fugitive! Grab him!"

Austin watched as a tangle of arms grabbed at the black man and yanked him from the closet. Angry hands clawed at the coarse sack he wore, and some even scratched his face and caught at his ears.

But it was the look in his eyes that made Austin cringe. He had seen a frightened horse rearing up in the street look like that, but never a human being. The black eyes were wild with panic.

"What are they going to do to him, Father?" Austin said.

The men in the crowd swooped down on the cowering black man and lifted him up onto their shoulders like a bag of potatoes. With the women all cheering "Stolen property!

8

Beat him!" the men hauled him off the stopped train.

Wesley Hutchinson brushed past Austin with his fists doubled and took off in their wake.

"Wesley, please be careful," Mother called after him.

Father appeared not to have heard her as he strode angrily down the aisle.

"Jefferson, you must stay here," she said, and this time she reached out her thin arms and grabbed him.

Austin followed Father past the empty seats and down the steps to the outside. By then the slave had been thrown down into the mud and was surrounded by a circle of men. They were all dressed like the most fashionable gentlemen of 1860, in their black wool frock coats and matching trousers. But their faces could easily have been those of common street criminals lurking in an alley. Every set of teeth was gnashed, every pair of eyes ablaze with cruelty. It made Austin shiver.

"Does he have a brand?" shouted one man.

Another man tore the sack away from the slave's quivering skin and cried out, "This darky is Singleton's!"

"A runaway, sure enough!"

"Just a moment!"

Above the bevy of southern drawls, Wesley Hutchinson's mid-Atlantic voice cracked like a whip. All heads turned, and beside him, Austin felt suddenly naked.

"If he's run away from a Carolina plantation, why is he on a train headed south?" Father shouted at them. "Wouldn't he go north?"

"Let's ask him!" the first man barked out. He leaned over the slave, who was curled up in a ball like a whipped dog. "Why *were* you aboard that train, boy?"

Boy? thought Austin. *He must be 20 years old. He's no boy!*

Man or boy, the slave didn't speak.

"Answer me, you cuffee!" the man cried. And he shot out his foot and kicked the slave in the side.

The black man bleated.

"Father! They're hurting him!" Austin whispered hoarsely.

"They won't do it again!" Wesley Hutchinson stepped forward and held out his hand to the slave. The slave didn't reach up.

"What, may I ask, are you doing?" said the white man. "This animal is a fugitive!"

"He is not an animal—he's a human being—created by God," Father said. "I defy any of you to lay a hand on him until you know what he is about here."

"I'll allow I know what he's about!"

That came from a whiny-voiced man with a thin beard who elbowed himself up from the back of the crowd. He was followed by a balding man who was growling.

"A slave I caught just the other day tried the same trick," the thin-bearded man said. "Ran just north of here to the last stop before Charleston—sneaked aboard there and thought he could stay on the train when it headed back north."

"You caught him, did you?" someone asked him.

An ugly smile split the bearded man's face. "Did you ever see one of these that could outsmart one of us?"

He pointed at the slave with his toe, and the crowd broke into laughter. The balding man growled.

I don't see what's so funny, Austin thought.

Father caught hold of the slave's wrist and pulled him to his feet. The laughter was cut off like someone had put a knife to its throat. The black man cowered.

"This *man* belongs to no one—except God Almighty,"

Father cried. "He was right to run for his freedom—and you are wrong to try to detain him!"

"Wrong?" the man with the thin beard shouted indignantly. "It's the law!"

"That which is not just is not law!" said Wesley Hutchinson. "William Lloyd Garrison wrote it, and I believe it! You're sinners—every one of you! Now if you will kindly step aside, I will escort the young man where he belongs."

But the men moved forward like a menacing wall.

"Who are you?" cried Baldy. He pointed straight at Father, who straightened himself to his full height, his hand still on the quivering slave's bare arm.

"I am Wesley Hutchinson. I've just arrived from the North."

"A Yankee," several people muttered suspiciously.

Thin Beard narrowed his eyes. "Are you an abolitionist?"

"Yes, I am," Father said, "and I am proud of it."

"Unhand that slave at once!" Thin Beard shouted. "I have a job to do!"

"It's the devil's job, then!" Father shouted back.

"Give him over, or you'll be hanged yourself!"

"Do that!" someone else cried. "Hang him!"

"No!" said another. "Grab the boy!"

Austin felt a pair of hands grab him from behind. He opened his mouth to scream, but at the same time, his feet came off the ground and one of the hands closed roughly across his lips.

"Let go of my son!" Father cried.

"Then you let go of the slave!" shouted the whiny voice over Austin's head.

Father kept his hands firmly on the slave's arm, but Austin could see his eyes wavering. Thin Beard let go with one hand and pawed around under his jacket while retaining his grip on Austin. When he pulled out his hand, it held something metallic and slender. Austin heard himself yelp as the man pointed it toward him. It was a shiny Colt revolver. The crowd hummed with admiration.

Slowly, Father loosened his hold on the slave. Austin felt himself being hurled forward, and his face was suddenly against his father's chest. From under Father's elbow, he could see Thin Beard and Baldy dragging the slave away. The crowd followed, roaring like a storm, with a few casting scornful looks at the Hutchinsons over their shoulders as they went.

"Are you all right, son?" his father said.

Austin stared after the crowd. "Where are they taking him? What will they do with him?"

"They'll probably take him to his 'owner,'" Father said bitterly. "What *he* does with him will depend on what kind of man he is. Though any man who would own another is no man at all as far as I am concerned." He pulled Austin to face him. "Are you sure you're all right? You just had a gun pointed at your head!"

"I just want to know—"

"All you need to know is what you saw," Father said. He glared across the train yard at the vanishing crowd. "Now you understand what your mother and I are fighting so hard for."

"Wesley," said a weak voice from the door of the train car. "Where is Drayton?"

For the first time since he'd followed his father off the train, Austin realized they were actually in Charleston.

Was Uncle Drayton one of those men in that mob? he thought. *Does he do things like that to his slaves?*

"Drayton!" Mother said suddenly, her voice lilting more

than ever. She gazed with tear-shiny eyes toward the station house. Emerging from the early morning shadows was a man taller than Father, wearing a long frock coat and trousers tucked into his knee-high boots. There was a wide-brimmed hat on his head, but the moment he spotted them, he pulled it off, and even from across the train yard, Austin could see a smile spread slowly across his face.

That's Mother's smile! Austin thought. *And his hair is the same color as hers! And mine!*

Sally Hutchinson held her arms out and nearly fell from the top step of the train. The man took the train yard in three long strides and swung her down like a little girl. An unfamiliar sound came out of her.

I've never heard Mother giggle before, Austin thought. *I didn't even know she knew how!*

"Drayton, it's really you!" she said through her laughter.

"How's my little sweet potato pie?" he said.

Drayton Ravenal set his sister down on the ground, and at once her knees buckled under her. Father rushed forward to grab her, and his arms got tangled up with Uncle Drayton's. But Austin saw it was their eyes that got into the worst knot. For an instant, it looked as if neither one of them would be able to get unsnarled enough to speak.

"Hello, Wesley," Drayton said finally.

He pronounced it "Wez-leh," and Austin's ears pricked up. He liked the way the man's voice sounded—it was even more silky than his mother's. He decided to start talking like that.

"Drayton," Father said tightly. "It was kind of you to meet us."

"Kind!" Uncle Drayton's eyebrows shot up, and Austin noticed for the first time that he had his and Mother's same brown eyes and their small, tilted-up nose. The only thing missing was Austin's freckles. "Kindness has nothing to do with it, sir!" Drayton said. "You all are my family. Who else would you expect to meet you when you're coming home? The rest of the family is waiting for you at the carriages."

"I thought perhaps you would send one of your 'boys,'" Father said.

There was an uncomfortable silence.

Austin twisted his toe in the mud.

"When are we going to your house?" Jefferson said.

For probably the first time in his life, Austin was happy to hear his brother whine.

"Now, who is this?" Uncle Drayton said.

"I'm Jefferson. Who are you?"

"Jefferson, really—your manners," Father said sharply.

"It's all right," said Drayton. "I expect it's been a long trip. You've all a right to be a little cranky."

Austin grunted. *Jefferson doesn't need a long trip to make him cranky. He can be that way before he even gets out of bed.*

"Ah, and this must be our Austin!" Uncle Drayton said in a voice that reminded Austin of honey. He took Austin's hand in both of his and looked into his face.

Uncle Drayton's skin was tanned brown and smooth, with only a neatly trimmed fringe of whiskers framing his chin. His eyebrows and hair looked as if they'd been combed with delicate little teeth, but there was a roughness about him that made Austin straighten his shoulders and hold up his chin.

"He looks like a Ravenal, Sally," Uncle Drayton said.

"He's a Hutchinson, born and raised, Drayton, and don't you forget it," Father said.

Austin saw only the faintest shadow of darkness go through his uncle's eyes. "I'm sure I won't forget that, Wesley."

Then Uncle Drayton scooped up Mother in his arms and looked commandingly around the train yard. Austin watched him raise his hand and flick his wrist, and suddenly there was a black man of about 20, dressed in an elegant blue uniform trimmed with gold braid, coming toward them and pulling a small wagon.

"These are your bags?" his uncle said, pointing to a pile the conductor had made on the ground.

Father nodded suddenly and leaned over to pick up two of them.

"Seton will get those," Uncle Drayton said.

"My sons and I are capable of handling our own baggage—"

"Wesley, please," Mother said.

Father snapped his mouth shut and let the bags go. But he didn't watch as Seton lifted them into the cart, muscles rippling under his jacket sleeve. Austin tried to catch the slave's eye to smile at him. Best to get acquainted with everyone right away. But Seton didn't meet his eyes.

It's probably because of what Father said, Austin thought. *I didn't expect him to be so rude.*

But he shrugged it off and grinned to himself. This was his chance to live a whole new life for a while, and nothing was going to keep him from enjoying every exciting minute of it.

✛ ✛ ✛

Chapter Three

Two emerald-green carriages waited at the other end of the train yard, both with gold scrollwork and mountings, each with a perfectly matched pair of horses. Austin had ridden in hundreds of carriages in his life, but none so fine as either of these.

"Are those broughams?" Austin asked, hoping he was getting the southern drawl in his voice.

The door to the first carriage opened and a short, almost-plump woman stepped out. She surveyed them with large, chocolate-brown eyes and pressed her lips together.

I hope this isn't Aunt Olivia, Austin thought.

He wasn't sure why. The woman, who was dressed in a pink gown and cape almost too wide to get through the carriage doorway, didn't look exactly mean. In fact, she hurried toward them holding out two ivory-colored hands to Mother as if she'd practiced doing it.

"Olivia, how wonderful to see you!" Sally Hutchinson said. "How long has it been?"

"I never think in terms of years!" Aunt Olivia said. "I don't like to remember how old I am!"

That's silly, Austin thought. *I know exactly how old I am every minute. Today it's 11 years, three months, and nine days.*

"Austin!" Mother said.

He looked up and found Aunt Olivia standing close to him—at least as close as her billowing dress would allow. Austin's thought this time was that she was soon going to have a double chin.

"Welcome to Charleston, Austin," Aunt Olivia said.

To his dismay, she bent forward and kissed his cheek. Fortunately, she moved quickly toward Jefferson.

"This is Jefferson," his mother said—a little nervously, Austin thought. And with good cause. When Aunt Olivia kissed Jefferson, he slapped her lip print off his cheek with a vengeance and wouldn't stop saying "Bleck!" even when Father planted his hand over Jefferson's mouth.

"What on earth is going on out here?" said a voice from the carriage.

A girl of about 13, as skinny as a flagpole, climbed out. She narrowed her close-together brown eyes—the color of mud, Austin decided—arched her long neck like a hungry stork, and then dismissed them all with a toss of the thin curls that straggled down the back of her neck. Behind her, seeming almost to be part of the skinny girl's gown, was a black girl the shape of a tree stump. The girl stood with her lower lip hanging down and her wide eyes blinking.

"Tot, hold my dress up!" the white girl said. "It's getting all muddy!"

Tot plucked the back of the blue flouncy skirt up in the air, exposing white pantaloons to the train yard. The white girl angrily slapped it down.

"Polly, honey, these are the Hutchinsons," Aunt Olivia said.

"Hello," Polly said coldly. She picked up the sides of her skirt herself with fingers that made Austin think of bird claws and moved dutifully through the group with Tot following her as if she were nailed to her. When Polly got to Jefferson, he leaped behind Father's pant leg and peered out at her with his eyes crossed and his tongue sticking out.

Austin stifled a groan. *Why does Jefferson have to be such a piglet about everything?* he thought. *No wonder this girl looks like she's been sucking on a pickle.*

It was obvious he was going to have to change her opinion of the Hutchinsons. He stuck his hand out.

"Don't pay him any mind," he said, once again trying to sound like Uncle Drayton. "We Hutchinsons aren't all like that. I'm Austin."

"Good for you," she said. And with a swish of pale-blue silk, she moved like a praying mantis to her mother's side. Tot silently mouthed the words "Good for you," and scurried to stand behind her.

Austin blinked.

"And here are our Kady and Charlotte," Aunt Olivia said. She sounded like she was weary of all these introductions.

At first, Austin saw only one girl. She must be 16-year-old Kady—slender and willowy, with rich-looking dark-brown hair. Her eyes were round and the color of honey, and she moved freely, instead of like someone had taught her how to walk. But although she looked curiously at Wesley Hutchinson, she seemed not to see Austin or the others.

"Nice to meet you all," she said faintly.

When she moved away from the carriage, Austin saw that

someone else was peeking out timidly.

"Oh, Charlotte, don't be ridiculous, honey," Aunt Olivia said.

Austin watched his youngest cousin as she stepped from the carriage.

Hey, he thought, *she looks like me.*

Charlotte Ravenal had wispy, deer-colored hair like his— though hers was pulled back from her face and cascaded silkily down her back. Her brown eyes were just like his, though he was sure his had never looked as shy as hers did. She even had a turned-up nose, peppered with freckles.

She sneaked a glance from under her fine little eyebrows, and Austin grinned at her. But she only nodded and hurried over to stand beside Kady.

Uncle Drayton cleared his throat. "Shall we be on our way, then? I'm so anxious for you to see our home."

"*Which* home?" Polly said. Behind her, Tot nodded several times.

Uncle Drayton shot her a look that Austin recognized right away. All fathers must use it when their children were saying more than they were supposed to.

"You'll have to excuse our Polly," Aunt Olivia said. "We *usually* stay in Charleston for all of January and February, the social season. She's a little disappointed."

It didn't look like Polly was the only one. For just an instant, Austin saw Aunt Olivia's eyes fall darkly on Uncle Drayton like a pair of shadows.

"Did you cut short your stay here because of us?" Austin's mother said.

"It was absolutely our pleasure to do it, potato pie," Uncle Drayton said briskly. "And if you give it another thought, there will be no pickled oysters for supper."

"Pickled oysters? Drayton—really?"

"I told Josephine before I left that we were to have as many as you could eat—and some of her cucumber preserves, too."

Once again, Austin watched in amazement as his mother turned pink and giggled. It took his mind off the dread he was feeling at the thought of eating pickled oysters and cucumber preserves.

The Ravenal girls and Austin's mother climbed into one carriage. Tot and a shriveled black woman named Mousie, whose only job seemed to be to give Aunt Olivia someone to order around, rode in a wagon with the bags. Austin wondered why Kady didn't have a girl, too.

Seton drove one carriage, while another black man with big, muscular arms drove the other. Uncle Drayton and Aunt Olivia joined Austin and Jefferson and their father in the second carriage, and Austin managed to get a seat next to his uncle.

"Now, then, Hutchinsons," Uncle Drayton said when they were on their way, "how was your journey? Long and uncomfortable, I'm sure."

"It was a good deal more than long and uncomfortable," Father said.

Austin looked uneasily at his father.

"Let me tell you what happened when we arrived in Charleston," Father said bitterly.

Suddenly, it was as if they were in a lecture hall in New York or Trenton, as Wesley Hutchinson stabbed at the air with his hands and told the story about the runaway slave.

Austin listened miserably. *It was a terrible thing, what happened to that slave,* he thought. *But why does Father have to spoil everything by talking about it?*

He turned to the carriage window and looked at the

streets of Charleston.

They're elegant streets, he decided at once. There were pastel-colored houses all lined up next to each other, each one boasting more lacy wrought-iron railings and wider porches than the one before it. Tall waving palm trees danced gracefully, and the magnificent church steeples pointed up into a blue sky untarnished by factory smoke.

I wonder why the lampposts are green. Why are all those people pouring into that hall with baskets on their arms? Oh, is that someone's house, that one with the Ionic columns? No, it has to be a hotel—

"You know, of course," Uncle Drayton said, "that we have divided South Carolina into districts called parishes. Charleston is in Christ's Church Parish." He pointed a graceful black-cuffed sleeve toward the window. "You'll see the Ashleh Rivah comin' up ahead. I have a little canal boat waitin' for us there to take us to St. Paul's Parish, where Canaan Grove is."

Ashleh Rivah? Austin studied that for a minute and then grinned to himself. Ashley River. He'd read that in Uncle Drayton's letter to the family. The plantation was situated right on it, about six miles from the city.

"One of two rivers on either side of Charleston," Uncle Drayton was saying. "The Ashley and the Cooper—" he pronounced it *Coopah* "—come together to form the Atlantic Ocean."

Austin cocked his head and frowned. "Don't you mean the two rivers flow into the ocean?"

Uncle Drayton gave a laugh that reminded Austin of a silver trumpet. "Just a little joke, Austin," he said. "We Charlestonians think pretty highly of our city."

"Yes, we do," Aunt Olivia snapped. "You know what you

did, don't you, Wesley Hutchinson, making that scene in the train yard?"

"I know what I was trying to do," he said. "I wanted that slave to have his freedom, as I do all of them."

Olivia waved that aside with a flap of her cape. "No, sir!" she said. "You let every one of those people in the train yard know that you are an abolitionist!"

"I'm not afraid," Father said. "I've had garbage thrown at me—"

"But I haven't, and neither has my family," she said shrilly. "I hope to heaven none of them finds out that your wife and sons are staying with us."

With one sour look over her shoulder, she turned her face to the window.

Now I know why I hoped that wasn't Aunt Olivia when I first saw her, Austin thought. *She doesn't want us here.*

Things didn't get much better once they were aboard Uncle Drayton's exquisite canal boat. All the women and girls went into the ladies' cabin behind a red velvet curtain. Father looked around the luxurious main cabin and said, "How many slaves did it take to build this, Ravenal?"

Uncle Drayton then immediately excused himself to go to the crew's cuddy. Austin was disappointed that he didn't ask him to come along.

But there will be plenty of other chances for us to get to know each other, he assured himself.

He pressed his face against a round window to get a look at the Ashley River. But the boat rocked gently, and before Austin knew it, his eyes were blinking sleepily closed. When they opened, Uncle Drayton was standing in the doorway.

"Canaan Grove just ahead," he said. "Anyone interested in catching a first glimpse of it?"

Austin didn't even answer. He burst across the cabin, already spewing out questions.

"How close are we?" he said. "Will I be able to see the rice mill from here?"

Uncle Drayton looked back over his shoulder as he pushed open the cabin door to the deck. "How did you know we had a rice mill?"

"Oh, I read all about rice plantations as soon as I knew we were coming," Austin said. "I know what to expect."

Uncle Drayton's mouth twitched. "Do you now?"

The boat rounded a graceful curve in the river, and Uncle Drayton pointed his long arm ahead.

"Canaan Grove," he said.

Austin felt his chin drop to his chest.

There, sprawled before them like an endless tapestry of velvety green, was the plantation. And it went far beyond what Austin had dreamed up in his own imagination.

The land came out to a point into the river, and at its tip were two large ponds, shaped like wings.

"What are those?" Austin said.

"I call them the Monarch Lakes. You know the monarch butterfly?"

"A North American species," Austin said. "Their larvae feed on milkweed."

Uncle Drayton's mouth quivered again. "Right," he said. "Now just beyond this narrow strip of land you see here, between it and the plantation itself—"

"Those are the rice fields!" Austin cried. "But they're just mud."

"It's winter," Uncle Drayton explained. "We've plowed under all the stubble from the harvest so the winter frost can make the soil richer."

"We?" said Wesley Hutchinson as he stepped out onto the deck. "Don't you mean *they*—your human laborers, your chattel?"

Austin moved away from them to the rear of the boat, out of the sound of their voices—Uncle Drayton's low and patient, Father's angry and high and getting higher.

I'm just going to shut them out, Austin decided stubbornly.

That wasn't hard to do, because the closer he got to the plantation, the more grand it appeared. That brick building would be the mill where they threshed and pounded the rice. From here, Austin could see a long, wide pond stretched out behind it—with swans cutting graceful V's behind them as they swam.

Austin moved to another part of the boat and gaped some more. Wide, elegant steps of plush grass moved up from the river like a magnificent entranceway, leading to an impressive brick house peaked with chimneys and shiny with large windows. Big spreading oaks shaded it from the high, wintry noon sun. They were winter naked, but their branches waved long clumps of curly gray stuff that looked like an old woman's hair.

Austin darted to the other side of the boat to Uncle Drayton's side. "What is that big building? And why do the trees have gray hair on them? Are they dying? Is it poisonous? May I touch it?"

"Please!"

Austin stepped back, stung. Uncle Drayton looked down

at him and at once gently squeezed his shoulder.

"Please forgive me, Austin," he said in a tight voice. "I have some things to tend to. Why don't you ask your father those questions? He seems to have all the answers."

Uncle Drayton nodded so politely and coolly that it made Austin shiver. He flung his arms over the railing and stared at the plantation as it grew greener and larger before him.

I'm not going to ask Father one thing! he thought. *He's gone and spoiled everything!*

Behind him, Wesley Hutchinson said, "The gray material you see hanging from the trees is called Spanish moss. It's actually a harmless fungus." He cleared his throat. "Is there anything else you want to know?"

Yes, why you want to ruin it all! Austin wanted to say. But he just shook his head. Neither of them said a word until the canal boat was being moored beside the rice mill.

"I'm going ashore!" a familiar squeal announced.

Austin and his father wheeled around to see Jefferson standing on the railing at the stern of the boat. His feet in their high-topped leather tie-shoes were planted on the board, and his chubby arms were held straight out from his sides.

And then the canal boat bumped lightly against the wooden pier, and Jefferson's arms flapped like a pair of hummingbird's wings.

"Jefferson—no!" Father cried.

Jefferson let out a scream and disappeared over the side. There was a leaden *kerplunk*. And then there was nothing.

✟ ✟ ✟

Chapter Four

esley Hutchinson leapt to the railing and peered into the water with panicked eyes.

"I'll get help!" Austin cried.

But his father was already whipping off his frock coat and throwing one leg over the railing. Austin raced for the main cabin. Behind him, he heard another heavy splash, and his heart throbbed in his throat.

"Help—someone!" he screamed. He dug back into his mind, to the books he'd read. What did sailors say when someone—? *"Man overboard!"* he shrieked.

Uncle Drayton sprang from the main cabin with Mother, Aunt Olivia, and Mousie on his heels. Seton and the other black man tore out of the cuddy. Austin was only vaguely aware that even Charlotte, Kady, Polly, and Tot came out to see. Uncle Drayton grabbed him by both shoulders.

"Good heavens, boy, there's no need to become hysterical!" he said.

"Yes, there is! Jefferson fell overboard and my father

26

went in after him!"

"Then he'll fish him out. It's not but seven feet deep."

"No, he *won't!*" Austin shouted at him. "Father can't swim."

Uncle Drayton looked at him blankly for a second before he nodded to the two black men. Together they picked up a long pole and stuck it into the water. Uncle Drayton went to the side and called out, "Wez-leh! Grab the pole!"

But there was so much thrashing about going on in the water, Austin himself barely heard him.

"*Do* something, Uncle!" he cried.

"Good heavens," Uncle Drayton said. He peeled off his coat and hoisted himself lightly up and over the railing. He entered the water with hardly a splash and reached out and grasped the flailing Wesley by the back of his shirt.

"Stop flapping or you'll drown us both!" he shouted.

The waters settled somewhat, and Uncle Drayton pushed Austin's father by the shoulders toward the pole the slaves held out for him. Father grabbed it, but he snapped his head around wildly.

"Where is Jefferson?" he cried. "He's gone under!"

"Help him, Drayton!" said Mother, looking as if she would collapse at any moment.

Without hesitation, Uncle Drayton dove beneath the murky surface of the water. Everyone on the deck watched with their breath sucked in. Austin clutched the railing.

When Uncle Drayton came up, he was empty-handed.

"He's drowning!" Wesley Hutchinson cried. He started to let go of the pole, but Seton reached down and grabbed his forearm with his huge hand.

"Let me go—my son is drowning!"

"And a lot of good you'll do him if you drown yourself!"

Drayton shouted. He dove again.

Aunt Olivia pressed herself against the railing beside Austin. "Drayton, come out of there! You'll freeze to death!"

Father struggled against Seton's hand and kept shouting, "Let me go, man—please!"

Uncle Drayton came up and shook his head.

Austin glimpsed the blue tinge of his lips as he took in another huge breath and disappeared under the water. It was as still as a graveyard as they waited, until a high-pitched screech echoed from beside the rice mill.

"Let me go, you little cuffee. Let me go!"

"Jefferson!" Austin cried.

Out from the rushes that surrounded the rice mill came a sturdy coffee-colored boy of about 12 with a box-shaped face and a pair of shiny boot-black eyes. He waded toward them with a squirming mass of legs and elbows in his arms.

"Thank the Lord!" Mother said as she went to sit down.

Father pulled himself up on the pole, and Seton and the other slave lifted him with it onto the bank. He stumbled clumsily through the reeds and reached out for Jefferson, who thrashed around even more as the boy handed him over.

"No!" he screamed. "I want to swim!"

Uncle Drayton swam to the shore and surveyed both Father and the squalling Jefferson with a deep scowl. "We need to get both of you into dry clothes," he said.

"I'm fine," Father said, his voice shaking. "We just need to take care of the boy."

"Tot!" Uncle Drayton barked.

"Yes, marse?" answered the black girl, still sewn to Polly's skirts. Austin winced. She had a voice like a fingernail being scraped down a tin pail.

"Take my nephew inside and get him dry and warm."

Tot looked at Polly, her bottom lip stuck out like a bench. Polly gave her a shove in the middle of her back. The black girl trudged heavily down the plank Seton had by now set up and took Jefferson from Father.

"Where is the young man who saved Jefferson's life?" Father said. "I want to thank him."

Austin looked around, but the boy had disappeared, and the only person who seemed the slightest bit interested in where he had gone was Charlotte. She broke away from Kady's side and leaned over the rail.

"He was just doing what was expected of him," Uncle Drayton was saying. "There's no need to thank him."

"Because he's a slave?" Father said.

"I will not discuss this with you, Wez-leh—"

"No, of course you won't! No one can discuss the slavery issue anymore without violence erupting. Why, right on the Senate floor, a Massachusetts senator was whipped by the cane of a South Carolina congressman!"

"That was a personal matter—"

"By heaven, it's *all* personal! We each have a personal responsibility to preserve this Union, and the only way we're going to do it is to ban slavery in the South the way we've done in the North. Then we'll have one nation with everyone equal, the way it was intended."

"Are we treated equal to the North?" Uncle Drayton shot back. Austin was surprised to see fire in his brown eyes. "We're tired of paying the North's debts and getting nothing in return!"

"Money is not the issue here! Slavery is a sin and if it continues, it will start a war."

"Don't come at me with all these high moral principles, Wez-leh. You Northerners have treated your free blacks horribly. I'd like to see one of them who lives as well as my colored here. If you had enough black bodies in the North to reduce their cost, I believe you'd have slaves, too."

"That is a lie and you know it," Father said icily. "I have spent most of my life preaching against slavery, and I would not own a human being if I were starving to death."

"How about your children?" Uncle Drayton said, just as coldly. "Wouldn't you purchase the necessary labor to feed your children, if that were the only way to survive?"

"I most certainly would not."

A cool smile appeared on Uncle Drayton's lips. "It seems to me that you're doing that very thing right now. My slaves are going to feed your children while they're here."

Father lurched forward, his hands balled into shaking fists. "They will do no such thing, Drayton Ravenal!" he cried. And to Austin's horror, he added, "I am leaving this place tonight—and my wife and my children are going with me!"

"Now, Wez-leh," Uncle Drayton said, his voice suddenly smooth-sounding. "Suppose we see you all inside where you can get dry and eat. Then perhaps—"

But Father stomped off toward the house, leaving Uncle Drayton shaking his head, and Aunt Olivia sniffing behind her fan, and Austin close to tears.

The other Hutchinsons were taken quickly up the velvet steps to the house and in the front door that faced the river, Mother in Seton's arms, Austin plodding unhappily behind.

Seton took them into a room right at the top of the stairs, where Mousie was opening the trunks and Tot was piling wood in the fireplace. It was a sunny room with a tall, four-poster bed that had rice carvings on its posts and two wing-backed chairs pulled up to the fireplace, done in the same red-and-white brocade pheasants as the bed hangings and draperies. A more luxurious room Austin had never seen.

And my mother isn't even going to spend one night in it, he thought angrily as he watched Seton set Mother in the middle of the bed and slip out.

"Mousie!" Tot said in her nail-on-a-tin-pail voice. "I can't get this fire goin'!"

"Get you some more wood, then," Mousie said.

"There's plenty of wood in there already," Aunt Olivia said from the doorway. She managed to get her pink gown into the room and peered over Tot's shoulder. "We don't need a big fire," she said. "And what are you doing, Mousie?"

"I's fixin' to unpack Miz Sally's trunks, missus."

"There's no need. She isn't staying."

"Now, Livvy," Mother said. "I'm sure as soon as Wesley cools down, they can work out their differences."

"I don't know about that," Aunt Olivia said—a little bit cheerfully, Austin thought. He sat down on one of the wing-backed chairs.

"This is more than just a difference of opinion," she went on crisply. "Wesley has insulted our way of life, and then made it seem as if Drayton has offended *him!*"

Mother shook her head, smiling slightly. "My sweet Wesley. Will he ever learn when *not* to speak his mind?"

"Good heavens!" Aunt Olivia cried.

Austin jumped and looked around, but her piercing brown eyes were pointed straight at him.

"What is it?" Mother said.

"Those dirty traveling clothes—on my good chair!"

Austin bolted from the seat and looked down at it. There wasn't a speck there as far as he could see, but Aunt Olivia went at it viciously with the palm of her hand. From the bed, Mother coughed.

"I think you have worse problems than that, Livvy," she said. "Is it my imagination, or is this room filling with smoke?"

All eyes went to the fireplace, where Tot was frantically fanning the fire with both hands and flames were inching their way toward the edge of the hearth.

"Water!" Aunt Olivia cried.

Mousie leapt to the washstand in the corner and grabbed the porcelain pitcher.

"Tot, smother it!" Aunt Olivia shouted at her as Mousie drenched the fireplace. "Use your apron—use your hands if you have to!"

Austin's mother coughed louder, and she sat up on the bed, gasping for air. Austin flung open a window and then snatched up a towel from the washstand.

"I need some water for this—for Mother's face!" he said to Aunt Olivia.

"Don't let it burn the rug, you worthless fool!" she cried.

Austin was stung. He took the towel to his mother and rubbed her back until the flames were finally put out, Tot was banished from the room, and Mother stopped coughing.

Olivia swished over to the bed. "I hope you didn't think I was talking to you when I said 'worthless fool'," she said to Austin. "I was referring to that clumsy girl. I wouldn't have her in the house if Polly weren't so attached to her."

"Is your rug all right?" Mother said.

Aunt Olivia went over to inspect it once more. "Yes, thank heaven. It came from the Orient, you know."

"What part?" Austin said automatically.

"I beg your pardon?"

"China? Japan? Thailand? There are a lot of countries in the Orient."

Aunt Olivia gave him a long look and said, "I know you're all tired, and you have even more traveling to do. I'll send up some soup so you can eat before you leave."

The Hutchinsons ate their she-crab soup in a stiff silence even Austin and Jefferson were afraid to break. Jefferson went mercifully to sleep on his mother's bed, and Father excused himself to go downstairs. Austin flopped himself down on Mother's bed, too, and moaned.

This was the way it was most nights, actually. Father was off talking about serious things with other serious people, and Jefferson was asleep in his mother's bed, to be carried to his own later, and Austin and his mother read together and talked about the day. And Mother, of course, answered his questions.

But tonight was different. This was the first time Austin had felt as if his heart were going to break.

"Father is going to make us leave," he said into the pillow.

"That was this afternoon," Mother said. "It's way past nine o'clock, and we haven't gone yet, have we?"

Austin pulled his face up. "But Father yelled at Uncle Drayton," he said. "He didn't yell that much when those rioters burned us out."

She ran a pale hand down his arm. "Your father was humiliated today. He had to do something to save face."

"You don't think Father meant it?" he said.

"I think he meant it when he said it. But he was ashamed. He's had to come here asking for Uncle Drayton's help, which is a wound to any man's pride. And then when he got here, it was Uncle Drayton who had to save his son from drowning—and him, too!" Mother shrugged her frail shoulders. "He had to fight back with the only weapon he has, and that is his passion about slavery."

"He said we were leaving," Austin said stubbornly.

"But I think he's downstairs in the library right now patching things up with Uncle Drayton."

"I wish I knew what they were saying."

His mother watched him thoughtfully. "I didn't know you wanted to be here so badly, Austin. The life your father and I have given you boys hasn't been the best, has it?"

Austin didn't answer.

"Come on, then," she said. "It's question time. I'm sure you have thousands tonight!"

"It doesn't matter, if we're leaving," Austin said.

"I think it does. Whether we stay or go—no knowledge is ever wasted."

Austin sighed. "If you grew up here," he said, "why don't you talk like them, with that accent?"

"The one you've been trying to imitate all day?" she said, grinning. "It faded away when I moved North."

"Why did you go?" Austin said.

"Because your wonderful father believed the same things I did, and I wanted to spend my life with him."

"But didn't your father have slaves?"

Mother's face clouded. "He did, and I never liked it, from the time I was a little thing."

"Did he treat them mean?" Austin said.

"Sometimes."

"I bet Uncle Drayton is never mean to his slaves."

She touched Austin's cheek lightly. "I suppose you'll have

to see that for yourself. You like Uncle Drayton, don't you?"

Austin nodded sadly. "I think he likes me, too, don't you?"

"Of course! Why wouldn't he?"

"Aunt Olivia doesn't. I don't think the girls do either."

"Give them time. They don't know what a wonderful person you are yet."

Austin let his back slump. "Will they get to?"

"Ask a different question," Mother said.

Austin thought listlessly. "Why do they call grown slave men 'boys'?"

"They think of them as children."

"Children they take care of," Austin said. "Uncle Drayton said his slaves live better than the blacks do in the North."

"But the black folks in the North are free, Austin," she said. "That's the difference." She lifted his chin. "How did you feel when you thought Aunt Olivia was calling you a 'worthless fool'?"

"Awful," Austin admitted. "I don't care! I want to stay!"

"You know," she said, her voice suddenly cheerful, "I don't think I'll be able to sleep tonight if I don't have some warm milk. Would you mind terribly going to the kitchen and seeing if Josephine will fix some?"

"She'll do that now?" he said. "In the middle of the night?"

"Yes," Mother said. "But of course, you should ask nicely."

"Because these are human beings," he said automatically.

Mother nodded. "You'll have to go out the back door to get to the kitchen," she said. And she smiled. "That's right past the library."

⁜ ⁂ ⁜

Chapter Five

*A*s Austin padded down the stairs, he heard the murmur of voices from behind the polished oak door to Uncle Drayton's library. Austin pressed his ear to the door.

"I can't talk to you when you're coming at me like a cannonball, Wez-leh," Uncle Drayton was saying.

There was a muffled grunt from Father.

"The way some of the planters treat their people is as sickening to me as it is to you," Uncle Drayton went on. "I would do away with slavery today if I could. But the South has to be allowed to do that its own way."

"And how is that?" Father asked.

"I hope our leaders can find a way to end our peculiar institution peacefully."

"Call it what it is, Drayton—slavery. It isn't a 'peculiar institution.' It's an evil, unchristian practice."

"Whatever we choose to call it, I will do all I can to see that your sons are untouched by it," Uncle Drayton said. "You have my word on that. I won't turn them into Southrons."

Austin held his breath. The pause in the library was so long that he could feel himself turning blue. Finally, Wesley Hutchinson spoke.

"See that you don't," he said. "I've done little enough for those boys. I don't want my leaving them here to be my worst mistake yet."

"Yes!" Austin whispered hoarsely.

There was an abrupt silence in the library.

"Did you hear something?" Uncle Drayton said.

Skidding across the floor on his bare feet, Austin charged for the back hall and slipped under one of the two sets of stairs that curved away from each other like wings. But there was someone already there, and she sprang up like a striking snake.

"You little sneak!" she said. "What were you up to?"

Austin gasped and backed away. It was Polly, with the inevitable Tot moving behind her. Polly's close-together eyes bore down on him so hard that he thought they would cross. *She must be playing a game,* he thought.

So Austin grinned at her and said, "Well, if the grown-ups don't tell us anything, we have to find out some way!"

Polly sniffed, and Tot echoed with a snort of her own. *"My* mother always thinks of me. Just tonight she told me something I think I'll share with you."

Austin's heart lifted. "I can keep a secret."

"Oh, it's no secret," she said. She tried to toss her limp curls, though they only lay like wilted stems at the base of her neck. For the first time, Austin saw her smile, her teeth slightly stained with brown at their edges. "My mother said she is frightened half out of her mind that you and your mother and that brat of a brother are here in this house even for one day."

"Why?" Austin said. "Jefferson really won't hurt anyone."

"I'm talking about your father and his ridiculous ideas."

"But my father isn't even staying—"

"It doesn't matter! He's an absolutist."

"Abolitionist."

"That's what I said. He's spouted off his mouth in front of our neighbors. That makes it dangerous for all of us here." Polly brought her hatchet-shaped face close to his. "My mother says she certainly hopes that if you stay, none of you Hutchinsons opens your mouth to anyone around here about your being abso-whatevers."

Austin stared at her with his mouth agape.

"Well?" she said. "Do you plan to keep quiet—or shall I tell Papa that you eavesdropped on his conversation?"

Austin's mind was a muddle, something that didn't happen often. *I just want to be friends,* he thought desperately. *And that's one thing I* don't *know anything about.*

But evidently, Polly did. He'd have to do it her way.

"If anyone finds out my father is an abolitionist," he said finally, "it won't be from me."

Once again Polly sniffed, and with Tot snorting behind her she turned on her heel and marched back through the hall to the main part of the house.

I guess Aunt Olivia isn't the only one who doesn't want us here, Austin thought. But then he opened the door and let the cool night air rush across his face. *That's all right. I can show them I'm not just like my father. I'm here to make friends.*

It was still dark the next morning when Austin felt a hand shaking his shoulder.

"Austin, son . . . wake up," his father said near his ear. "It's time."

Austin came straight up in the bed with his head reeling. "No, Father," he said, his mouth still clumsy with sleep, "I'm staying. Aren't I?"

"I've just come to say good-bye," Father said.

"Oh." Austin felt himself cave in with relief. He pushed back the covers and put his feet over the side of the bed. "I'll come and see you off, then," he said.

Moments later, he was in his clothes and shoes, following his father down the massive front steps of the Ravenals' mansion toward the carriage that waited on the drive. The two white horses stomped sleepily and blew frosty air out of their nostrils, and beyond them the river stood dark and silent beneath the swaying Spanish moss. Austin smiled.

Those horses are taking Father to meet his train, he thought, *but I'm staying here with the river and the moss and everything else that will soon feel like it belongs to me, too.*

He followed his father down a few steps, and then Father stopped. He turned and said, "I'm depending on you to help take care of your mother and Jefferson."

"I will," Austin said.

"It's going to be a little harder now—and more important than ever."

"I *know*," Austin said. "I'll be fine."

For a moment, a shadow seemed to fall across his father's face, leaving his eyes sad and shimmery in the gathering light.

"I want you to remember what you saw in the train yard yesterday," he said. "Slavery has become so necessary here that it has ceased to appear evil to these people. Don't lose sight of that. You may look like a Ravenal, but you have been raised like a Hutchinson. My grandfather Thomas never had a slave—"

"He didn't need them. He was a doctor," Austin said impatiently.

"But my father, Taylor Hutchinson, wasn't. He ran his plantation without owning one other human being."

"And didn't you say he sold off all the land because he couldn't keep it up anymore?"

"He did, and I am proud of that," Father said. "A way of life is no substitute for the rights of people."

Austin nodded automatically, and he shivered. It may have been the South, but it was cold that time of morning.

"You need to get inside," his father said. "I will come back as soon as your mother is well enough to travel again—or when, God willing, slavery is done with and we can have a home again, the four of us. Keep that in your prayers to our Father, Austin."

With that he turned briskly and strode to the carriage and got in without looking back. Austin watched as the carriage disappeared into the trees.

Now I know I'm here to stay for a while! he thought.

But oddly, the thought didn't make him feel happy. He suddenly wanted to run after the carriage and say good-bye one more time, and maybe ask another question or two. There was a painful pinching in his chest.

Why do I feel sad? he thought. *Father never really seems very near anyway—even when he's right there.*

He wasn't like Uncle Drayton, whose presence filled a room even after he left it.

And I have Ravenal in me—lots of it, Austin thought. He

let himself into the Big House. *I belong here now. I have a real home now.*

"Why do we have to go to church today?" Austin said later that morning. "We never go to church."

"That's because we are hardly ever near a church on a Sunday," Mother said. "We're almost always between towns, riding on something with wheels."

She bit off the thread she'd been using to sew the torn foot strap back onto Austin's dark-blue trousers. He stood in the middle of her room in his drawers, shirt, and waistcoat, wrapping his Windsor tie around his hand and unwrapping it again.

"I already know the Lord's Prayer and the Ten Commandments," he said, "and I can recite all the books of the Bible—even backward if you want—so what do I need to go to church for? Why can't we just have prayers here with you like we always do? You're too sick to go anyway."

Mother tossed him the trousers and flicked her eyes toward the door. Jefferson was just letting himself in, smoothing his chubby hands down over his new pantaloons.

"I've been to church once, Mother," Austin said, as Jefferson hoisted himself up onto the bed to listen. "And it was so boring I kept falling asleep. Don't you remember Father poking me because I was drooling on his sleeve?"

Jefferson giggled. Mother frowned.

"Austin, please," she said, watching Jefferson's face with an anxious look on her own. "It's what they do here. If you want to learn everything about this place, then you ought to go to church. It's part of their life."

"That wasn't the part I wanted to learn about," he said stubbornly.

"Me neither!" Jefferson said.

Mother closed her eyes. "There will be a fit pitched here if you make a scene, Austin."

She nodded at the top of Jefferson's head. Austin scowled at it.

Just once I would like to do something I want to do without having to think about him, he thought.

His mother lay back on the pillows and started to cough from way down low. Austin sighed.

"All right," he said. He grabbed Jefferson's hand and yanked him off the bed. "Come on, shrimp. What do we do, Mother?"

"Go downstairs for breakfast," she said.

A surprise awaited him in the dining room. There were 40 black children standing around the table. Each one wore a long shirt of sackcloth down to his or her knees with no visible pants or even any shoes, just like the children he'd seen from the train, and each held a mussel shell in one hand. They all appeared to be holding their breath like they were waiting for something.

Also in the room were Uncle Drayton and the rest of the Ravenals, watching.

Just then the door to the pantry swung open and a large black woman with hips as wide as the doorway swished in with a tray above her head. Stumpy Tot was behind her, struggling to tote just as big a load.

"Now don't nobody go grabbin' nothin' till I get these victuals on the table," the woman said.

"That's right, Josephine," Uncle Drayton said from his pose by the fireplace next to Aunt Olivia. "There will be no grabbing and wolfing at the Ravenal table."

There were pots of cocoa, plates of golden biscuits, and platters piled high with eggs, sausages, potatoes, and buckwheat pancakes. The children dug their shells into the food like spoons.

It doesn't look like Uncle Drayton treats his coloreds so bad to me! Austin thought.

As Tot slid the last of the platters of eggs onto the table, the tray dipped and the big plate bounced against the table edge and flipped over onto the floor.

Jefferson made a dive for the mess. Austin grabbed him by the shoulder.

"I'm hun-gry!" Jefferson cried. "I *want* some of that!"

"Jefferson, come here," Uncle Drayton said. He crouched down and held out his arms.

Jefferson surveyed him suspiciously and then shot across the room into Uncle Drayton's arms. He held the boy high up over the table.

"These are our colored folks' children," Drayton said. "They come in here to have breakfast every Sunday so we can make sure that everyone is growing up healthy."

"Is that why you're watching them eat?" Jefferson said.

For once the little shrimp is right, Austin thought. *Aunt Olivia and Kady and Polly all look like they're inspecting them.*

Only Charlotte took no interest. She sat on a side chair under the window, swinging her legs so that the bottom ruffles of her drawers and several of her petticoats showed.

"Everyone seems to have a good appetite today, don't they, Jefferson?" Uncle Drayton said.

"Not that one," Jefferson said, pointing and shaking his curls.

Austin followed his finger to a figure near the other end of the table. It was the boy who had saved Jefferson from drowning in the river the day before. If Jefferson recognized him, he didn't show it.

Aunt Olivia moved to the boy's side. He didn't look up at her but kept his eyes fixed on his still-full plate.

"Are you sick?" she said.

The boy raised his eyes to look straight ahead of him and shook his head.

"Answer me!" she said.

"No, missus."

"Then why aren't you eating?"

"Ain't hungry, missus."

"Look him over, Kadydid," Uncle Drayton said.

Kady moved in from the green sideboard and silently waited for the boy to get out of his chair. He stood before her without a word while she took him by the shoulders and studied his face.

They really care about these children, Austin thought. *That's just the way my mother would look at me if I were sick enough not to eat. If Father had stayed here and looked around, he might change his mind about slavery!*

"He seems fine to me, Papa," Kady said, patting the boy on the shoulder.

"Nonsense!" Aunt Olivia said. "A boy of—how old are you?"

"Twelve, missus," he said.

"A boy of 12 not eating the best meal of his week? Something is not right."

Aunt Olivia tapped Kady aside and thrust her hands against the boy's abdomen. Immediately, her large eyes turned to thunderstorms.

"What is *this?*" she said. Without warning, she jerked his shirt up, revealing a pair of skimpy drawers. She gave those a yank, too, and out fell four golden-brown biscuits to the floor. She gave the sturdy boy a shake, though he barely moved. "What were you doing with these in your clothes?"

"Perhaps he was saving them for later."

It was Charlotte who had spoken. Her voice was surprisingly clear, but she kept her eyes fixed firmly on the floor.

"There is only one way to settle this," Aunt Olivia said. Her voice was brisk with impatience as she looked at the boy. "If you want these biscuits, boy, eat them now."

The boy stared at them on the floor like forgotten toys and said, "No thanks, missus."

"He doesn't want them," Uncle Drayton said. He looked over the table with a smile. "Who does?"

Several hands waved, including Jefferson's.

"You can't eat them, silly," Polly said to him. "They're dirty now." Then she deposited them onto four of the slave children's plates.

"What is your name, boy?" Uncle Drayton said.

The black lad cocked his head as if he were actually considering not answering. Even Austin had picked up by now that a slave answered all questions promptly and added *marse* or *missus* if those questions were asked by the master or his wife.

"Henry-James Ravenal," the boy said finally. Austin saw a wide space between his two front teeth.

"Ria's boy," Aunt Olivia said. "Daddy Elias's grandson."

"All right," said Uncle Drayton. "Tell his mama he's off his feed. Will my family join me in the drawing room now for our breakfast?"

Austin really didn't want to leave the dining room. The black children here looked friendlier than the people he was going to eat with. Certainly they'd make better friends than sour-faced Polly and always-serious Kady. He fought down a rising ache of disappointment as he followed them and slid into a chair next to Charlotte. She didn't look at him as she took up her fork and picked at her food.

✦ ✦ ✦

Chapter Six

efore the carriage could be boarded for the ride to church, there was a great deal of whining from Polly and grousing from Aunt Olivia about the way their dresses were going to get wrinkled.

"Polly, for heaven's sake, what does it matter?" Kady said. "After an hour in church, your dress will be wrinkled anyway."

An hour? Austin thought woefully. *We have to sit there for an hour?*

To Austin's surprise, Uncle Drayton turned to him. "Austin, my friend, how would you like to be Seton's assistant whip today?"

"You mean . . . sit up in the coachman's seat with him?"

"That's what I mean. Climb on, and let's be on our way."

Austin bolted down the steps toward the carriage, grabbed on to the side and tried to pull himself up. In his sweaty-handed excitement, his fingers slid off and he started to fall backward. Seton's muscular arms caught him and lifted him like a flaky biscuit onto the driver's seat.

"Clumsy thing, isn't he?" Olivia said from inside the carriage.

47

"I don't mind that so much," Polly said. "It's the constant talking that is going to make us all crazy. He asks more questions than a first reading primer!"

"And in that way he has," Aunt Olivia added with a sniff. "You'd think he was a college professor from Massachusetts."

"Boston Austin—that's what I'll call him!" Polly said.

Austin tried to concentrate on the scenery they were passing. On his side of the coach there was grass sticking up out of shallow water like thick, unruly hair, and nosing their way up through it from time to time were wooden stubs that reminded Austin of knees. There were trees growing out of this muck, too, with bottoms that spread out like bells. Leaves lay on top of the water, slimy in the sun.

"What is that?" he said to Seton.

"That there's a swamp," Seton said in a deep, rich voice. "Lot of them in this here low country."

"What are those things that stick up?"

"They's cypress knees."

"And that really tall grass—with the funny tassels on top?"

"That's pampas grass. Cut you like a knife if you go runnin' through it."

Austin felt a little chill of excitement. Go running through it. That's what he'd come here to do—go running through something, have adventures. . . .

He sagged a little against the carriage seat. If he could only get to spend time with Uncle Drayton and show him how eager he was to learn. Or if he could get to be friends with . . . who? It was certain *Polly* didn't care much for him.

He felt something warm against his palm and looked down. Seton had reached over and was picking up Austin's hand and placing the reins in it.

"What am I doing?" Austin said.

"Looks like you drivin' the coach, Massa Austin."

Austin looked down at his hand and then at the two chestnut mares ambling calmly up the road.

"I *am* driving!" Austin said. "I'm doing a good job!"

"How long you been drivin', Massa Austin?" Seton said.

"I've never driven before!"

"Naw! You funnin' me."

Austin shook his head proudly. "No, I've never driven a coach before today."

"Then I'll allow you just got a gift for it, is all."

Austin sat up straighter in the seat and grinned.

"Now, I s'pose you oughta put both hands on the reins now 'cause we gonna turn at this here crossroads we comin' to."

Austin's fingers tightened around the reins. "How do I do that?"

"You just say, 'haw'. Good an' loud now, like you's hollerin' at your little brother."

Austin grinned. "I can do that!"

"You do it, then—do it now."

"Haw!" Austin yelled.

To his delight, the two horses tilted their heads to the left and smoothly rounded the turn. Austin gave a squeal that outsquealed Jefferson himself. His hands automatically jerked the reins as he did, and the horses came up with a start. Their hooves skidded, spewing mud in all directions and causing the carriage to lurch to the side. A chorus of muffled shrieks erupted in the back. Seton swiftly took the reins from Austin.

"Gittup now!" Seton called out. "Gittup!"

The horses moved forward again, lifting their legs high to make up for lost time. The carriage righted itself, and the ride continued smoothly.

"I wasn't supposed to pull the reins, was I? I've read about it in books, but it's different when you're really doing it."

Seton chuckled. "Don't you let it worry you none, Massa Austin," he said. "I reckon our folks needs a little shakin' up now and again."

Austin bit his lip. "Do you think Uncle Drayton is ever going to let me drive again? I was counting on him teaching me to ride a horse."

"We ain't gonna say a word about this to Marse Drayton."

Austin felt his eyebrows come to life. "You mean lie?"

A shadow fell across Seton's face. "You ever been 'round slaves, Massa Austin?" he said.

Austin shook his head.

"Then you let me take care o' this," Seton said.

It was only a few minutes more until they reached the church. When Seton pulled the coach up to a rectangular, salmon-colored building, Austin made a quick decision.

When church gets really boring, he told himself, *I'll just imagine I'm driving a team of four horses—no, six!—and they're about to run away with the coach, with Polly and all the Ravenals in it!*

He was just trying to make up his mind whether to save only Charlotte and maybe Kady when someone said, "Well, are you coming or not?"

Austin looked down at Polly. She was standing on the ground below, peering at him from under her pork-pie hat. Her mud-colored eyes were narrowed in impatience. Austin noticed that it was the first time he'd seen her without Tot sewn to her like a pocket. That was probably only because all the slaves had followed them on foot.

Austin climbed down and started to follow Uncle Drayton and Aunt Olivia. Polly grabbed him by the shoulder.

"I want you to remember, Austin Hutchinson," she said, "there will be no asking your questions during church—or trying to impress us with how much you know."

"I can't do that anyway," Austin said. "I don't *know* anything about church."

Polly's face cut open into a scornful smile.

"Are you some kind of heathen?" she said.

Austin shook his head, which he was sure was by now red up to the roots of his hair. "I believe in God! I say my prayers every night—and my father prays with us every day."

"Have you been baptized?"

Austin felt his mouth slowing. "I don't know—"

"You don't *know?*" Polly rolled her eyes and gave the veil that hung from the back of her hat a toss. "You're even worse than I thought."

With that, she plucked up her silk plaid ruffles and hurried off importantly after her family. Austin stood with a stinging in his chest.

"Come on, Austin!" said a voice at his side. It was Jefferson, tugging at his wrist. "Uncle Drayton says to hurry up. Don't you know the service is about to start?"

"*Yes,*" Austin snapped at him. He jerked his arm away from Jefferson and took him by the back of the collar.

"We have to be quiet in here," Jefferson said as Austin half-dragged him past the walled cemetery toward the church.

"Oh, hush up, Jefferson," Austin said.

Jefferson sniffed. "My name isn't Jefferson anymore. It's Little Man. That's what Uncle Drayton calls me." He looked up at Austin with his blue eyes wide. "What does he call *you?*"

"Hush up," Austin said again.

St. Paul's Church was bigger on the inside than it looked on the outside, and Austin saw that it was much sunnier and more cheerful than the dark, musty church he'd been to that one Sunday in Baltimore. The windows that lined the walls let in streams of winter sunlight that shone against the polished wood of the pews.

Austin followed the Ravenals up a side aisle to a pew at the front and dumped Jefferson unceremoniously onto the seat. Then he sat down and turned to have a look around. Above them on both sides and behind were balconies filled only with black faces, still and silent as if they were waiting for something important to happen.

"It isn't polite to turn around and look behind you in church!" Polly hissed to him.

She just talked across two people to tell me that, Austin thought as he turned back around. *And nobody's telling her to hush up!*

Just then, Austin heard music from an organ. The people were suddenly on their feet, and from up in the galleries Austin felt a ripple of movement and excitement. He had to gnaw on the inside of his mouth to keep from asking, "What's going to happen?"

He got his answer anyway. The organ paused, the congregation seemed to take one big breath, and the place was suddenly filled with a song.

"Blessed be the tie that binds our hearts in Jesus' love. . . ."

Voices boomed and piped and trilled all around him.

"The fellowship of Christian minds is like to that above. . . ."

Kady's came out full and crisp and clear.

"Before our Father's throne we pour united prayers. . . ."

Behind him a man sang right through his nose.

"Our fears, our hopes, our aims are one. . . ."

But Austin's ears were drawn more to what was happening in the galleries.

As the song went on, the black folks began to sway, as if they were one person.

Someone on the left side started slapping a rhythm. Someone on the right sang out an "Alleluia." Heads bobbed, voices hummed between the words, and eyes closed as if they were experiencing some special pleasure they wanted to save in their minds.

Austin didn't close *his* eyes. He couldn't take them off the slaves.

They look happy, he thought. *They don't look like someone's treating them like animals at all!*

He was sorry to hear the song end, and he sat down reluctantly. Jefferson squirmed and said hoarsely, "Is it over?" Down the row, Polly leaned forward and glared.

Austin smothered Jefferson's mouth with his hand and clamped his wriggling body next to him. It was clear Polly was going to pick on him no matter what, but he didn't want Uncle Drayton to get after him. Austin fixed his eyes on the man who was now standing up on the platform in front.

"Welcome to St. Paul's, my friends," said the white-haired man. "I shall read to you today from the Gospel of Luke."

There was a murmur from the galleries.

That's the third book of the New Testament, Austin thought. *What's so exciting about that?*

The man licked his fingers, turned a page, and began to read. In the balconies, everyone was leaning forward. Down the row, Aunt Olivia was patting her hair net. Polly was smoothing her skirt. Uncle Drayton was staring at the ceiling.

Only Kady and Charlotte seemed to be paying attention. Jefferson certainly wasn't. He sighed loudly and began to look around with a familiar gleam in his eye. Quickly, Austin reached inside his jacket and pulled out two marbles. They were made of hardened clay, and he'd found them at the last inn they'd stayed in.

He opened Jefferson's plump, sweaty hand and stuck the marbles in his palm. Jefferson sat back hard in the seat and passed them from one hand to the other, brow furrowed in concentration.

By now the man—whom Austin assumed was the minister, Reverend Pullens—had finished the story and closed his Bible. "That is one of my favorite stories of our Lord Jesus," he said, "because in this story, Jesus is a *man*."

Jesus, Austin thought. *That's God in the form of a person coming down to earth.* He'd heard about that.

He fidgeted with his jacket button. Yes, it was going to be boring, just like he thought. His father talked about God the Father all the time, and of course Austin believed in Him. But God the Father was like his human father—very far away. It was hard to be interested in *anything* Austin couldn't learn facts about in hopes of someday seeing it.

"Now, I know my favorite part of Jesus is supposed to be His perfect words and His perfect love," the minister went on. "But I can't help but love Jesus most as the *man*—come here among us to, well, throw a temper tantrum!"

There was a chorus of enthusiastic agreement from the galleries. The minister raised his voice, and his face was shining.

"Jesus went into the temple to pray and worship—just the way you've done today, my friends. Surely you didn't expect to find your neighbors selling their crops and their animals in our aisles, did you?"

"No, sir," the slaves murmured. "No, sir!"

"Neither did our Lord Jesus! But, my friends—" his voice lowered almost to a whisper as he said his next words sadly "—that is exactly what He found and it made Him *angry,* just the way you and I would be!"

Heads in the balconies nodded. The minister's voice rose again as he pointed to his own chest.

"Jesus was spitting mad down to the pit of His soul. And He turned those tables over and threw their evil wares right to the floor of the temple!"

Austin was a little interested. *Jesus did that?*

"Don't you think, my friends," Reverend Pullens said, "that Jesus still sees the likes of selling wares in the church? Don't you think He sees the evil things that still go on?" His gentle eyes sagged as if he were disappointed. "And don't you think when those evil things are done to you—don't you think He stands right behind you and He hurts for you? Yes, He *aches* for you—and He wants to turn over those tables for you right now. He's right there at your shoulder!"

Austin turned around with a jerk. He almost expected to see a man with disappointed eyes, right there.

What he did see was a woman with big cheeks looking bewildered and suddenly reaching down to swat at her feet. Austin realized two things at the same time. There was something bothering her ankle—and Jefferson was no longer on the seat beside him.

✝ ✞ ✝

Chapter Seven

The man Jesus forgotten for the moment, Austin lurched forward to bend his head between his knees and peer under the pew bench. Crouched in a ball, ready to spring at the hem of the lady's skirt, was Jefferson.

"What are you doing?" Austin hissed at him.

"I dropped one of my marbles."

Austin could feel his face going crimson. "Where is it?"

Jefferson pointed toward the lady's bottom ruffle and to Austin's horror began to reach toward it. With a lunge, Austin grabbed for Jefferson's hand. He caught it neatly and began pulling, but his little brother's palms were slippery with sweat, and he slipped out of Austin's grasp like a fish flopping free. Caught off balance on the seat, Austin went off the edge and landed with an echoing thud on the stone floor. He watched helplessly through his own knot of arms as Jefferson slid his hand under the edge of the lady's skirt and pulled it out, triumphantly displaying the clay marble.

"Now get up," Austin spat at him.

Jefferson crawled calmly out from under the seat and settled himself on the pew. Austin surfaced after him, brushing the dust balls from his dark-blue jacket.

"He is there—the living spirit of Christ!" Reverend Pullens said.

"Amen!" the slaves said.

"Quiet!" Aunt Olivia said.

Austin looked up to see her stabbing dagger eyes at him. But they didn't cut him as deeply as the disappointed look on Uncle Drayton's face.

During a dinner of ham and sweet potato pie, everyone seemed to talk around Austin. No one said a word to him, even about falling off the seat in church. By the time the long-awaited pandowdy arrived with its apples and sugar bubbling in a crust, Austin wasn't hungry anymore.

I'll just have to talk to Uncle Drayton and explain it to him, is all, he decided as the dishes were cleared away and the family scattered from the dining room. *When I tell him how it is with Jefferson, he'll understand. I bet he would even understand if I explained about the carriage.*

He decided against that. Seton had said he could take care of it. Austin had enough to worry about with getting this matter cleared up.

Uncle Drayton and Aunt Olivia had gone into the drawing room for tea, and Austin marched straight there. He was about to knock when Aunt Olivia's shrill voice shot out into the hallway.

"You told me this was going to be just fine, Drayton," she said.

"I did," said Uncle Drayton. He spoke in a quieter voice,

but it was so deep that it seemed to slide under the door like thick molasses.

Austin tiptoed to the stairs and tucked himself underneath.

"Those boys are *not* going to be fine here!" Aunt Olivia went on. "That Jefferson has my nerves in a frazzle—and the other one talks incessantly, Drayton."

"The boy does have a great deal to say."

"And that isn't the whole of it! It's the way he says it, as if he knew everything and the rest of us were mere imbeciles—idiots!"

"It's easy to see why that is," Uncle Drayton said. "It's that sniveling whiner Wesley. The poor child is following in the footsteps of a person so wrapped up in his noble causes that he hasn't time to be a man himself, much less teach his son how to be one."

Austin felt as if he were frozen to the floor. He wanted to run before he heard any more, but he couldn't move.

"You certainly aren't going to try to teach him, are you?" Aunt Olivia said.

"I had planned on it. Sally asked me—"

"I don't want them here that long. As soon as the other planters discover he and Jefferson are Wesley Hutchinson's abolitionist sons, we'll all be in danger."

"I have promised Sally that I would look after them until she's strong enough to travel again," Uncle Drayton said, "and that's exactly what I'm going to do. It's family."

"What do you intend to do, then?" she said stiffly.

"See that they are properly schooled. Polly can look after Jefferson."

"Polly is not going to be happy—"

"As for Austin—"

Austin held his breath. Here it came . . . Uncle Drayton's plan to teach him hunting and riding and the work of the plantation—to save him from being sniveling and whining.

"I have to go back to Charleston for several days. While I'm gone, I will put him in with Charlotte. Kady is doing a fine job with her, and that should be enough for the boy for the time being."

Austin was shaking his head hard. *No, Uncle Drayton,* he wanted to cry, *I don't want to learn to write my letters like a girl and drink tea! I want to go with you!*

I'll beg, he thought. *Surely if he knows how much I want—*

Just then the back door opened and heavy boots made their way across the hall.

"Marse Drayton want to see me?" said a deep, rich voice.

"That's what he say," answered a fingernail-scratching one.

Austin would have covered his ears if he hadn't recognized the first voice as Seton's.

"This here's Sunday," Seton said.

"I know," Tot whined. "Miss Polly got me workin', too."

Austin poked his head out cautiously as Tot dashed off, barefoot, up the stairway, and Seton tapped timidly on the drawing room door.

When he disappeared inside, closing the door after him, Austin could hear only murmurs at first. And then Uncle Drayton's voice rose, loud enough to send Austin back under the steps.

"You know I cannot abide a lie, boy!" he roared.

"This ain't no lie, Marse Drayton," Seton said. "I jus' wrenched too hard on them reins, and them horses, they just stop dead in the middle of the road."

"Nonsense!" said Aunt Olivia. "You are the best driver in the parish. You could never make such a stupid mistake."

"I reckon I can, missus. You be tellin' me all the time how stupid I is."

"Are you being insolent?" Uncle Drayton barked.

"No, sir, Marse Drayton. I don't even know what that means."

"Too big for your britches," Austin mumbled. His father had warned him about that many times.

"Well, see if you know what *this* means," Uncle Drayton said. "You know I am not a violent man, but if there is another accident with that carriage or those horses, you will pay dearly. Do not ever think that just because you are my body slave you can take liberties not allowed the others. The young ones watch you—I had one this morning who refused to show the proper respect right in my dining room. I expect you to set an example."

"Yes, Marse Drayton."

"Now you go see that those horses are warm and dry and the carriage cleaned."

"Isaac done took care o' that, sir."

"Did I say Isaac? *I—said—you!*"

Austin cringed under the steps. The door flew open and heavy boots clattered across the hall and out the back door. Austin waited until the drawing room door closed again before he slipped out after him. As he went, he heard Aunt Olivia say, "The darkies didn't used to be this much trouble, Drayton. What is happening?"

"Send for Charlotte, Olivia," he answered as Austin left the house. "I want to speak with her."

The big black man was already halfway across the yard

when Austin got outside.

"Seton!" he cried. "Wait!"

Seton slowed down, but he didn't stop. "I'm sorry, Massa Austin," he called back. "I gots to go."

Austin tore down the steps and down the drive, heaving for air when he caught up. "I know," he said. "I was listening under the steps. Why didn't you tell Uncle Drayton I was the one who was driving the carriage when it nearly turned over?"

Seton kept his eyes straight ahead as he strode on. "I done tol' you I wouldn't."

"But why should you get in trouble for something I did?"

Seton took a sharp turn toward a pole fence surrounding a long brick building that smelled of leather and animals. "I'd have got in trouble anyways. No point both of us sufferin'."

Seton leapt lightly over the fence, and Austin scrambled clumsily up onto it.

"But I don't understand why," Austin called to his back. "You didn't do anything wrong!"

Seton stopped and turned slowly to face him. His kind black eyes were smoldering. "A slave don't got to do nothin' wrong for to get punished. Now if you'll 'scuse me?"

He turned to go again, and Austin clung to the fence. "I'm sorry, Seton!" he called out. "I'm really sorry."

"Don't let it worry you none," Seton said. And then he disappeared into the building.

But it did worry Austin. He set off walking, his heart as heavy as his feet. He went through a stand of trees swaying with Spanish moss and surrounded by shrubs that flowered bravely in the winter chill. By the time he reached a brick building with a bubbling sound coming from inside, he was stumbling and breathing hard. He was glad to stop when the pond sprang up in his path. He flopped down and stared at it.

Two black swans swam silently by. Across the pond a white-tailed deer emerged from the woods and stared at Austin, unafraid.

Austin watched without interest. He'd wanted friends and he'd wanted Uncle Drayton to like him and teach him things his own father couldn't. Now he'd messed up both. Seton had gotten in trouble because of him. And Uncle Drayton . . .

Uncle Drayton hadn't meant he was *never* going to teach him to be a man, had he? Maybe he was waiting for Austin to show him he wasn't—what had he said?—a sniveling whiner—

Like his father.

Austin felt a pinch in his chest. Was that what Father was, really?

From somewhere off behind him, in the direction of the brick building where he'd left Seton, a deep voice suddenly began to sing out into the wintry air.

"Rabbit in the briar patch," it wailed. "Squirrel in the tree. I'd go huntin' by the river tonight, if I was free."

There was something urgent in the singer's voice that made Austin sit up and listen.

"I'd go huntin' by the moon tonight, take the squirrel right out of the tree. Down by the river tonight. But I ain't free."

It should have been sung sadly, but it sounded almost hopeful, and somehow it made Austin feel hopeful, too.

I'll show Uncle Drayton, he told himself firmly. *I'll find a way to fit here. He'll see. He'll just see.*

✛ ⚜ ✛

Chapter Eight

ustin found Kady and Charlotte out in the side yard the next morning under a poplar with their skirts poofed out around them. Although it was late January, the air was only slightly chilly, and the sun burned warmly through it from a cloudless blue sky.

"Good morning, Austin," Kady said. "Why don't you sit down and join us? We've a blanket here so you won't soil your clothes."

"Oh, I don't care about that!" Austin said and flopped down on the grass in as manly a fashion as he could manage. He could feel the dew seeping through his trousers.

"Charlotte was going to read to me from the *American Primer.*"

"Oh," Austin said.

"Is something wrong?" Kady said.

"No. It's just that . . . I finished the primer years ago."

"What do you read, then?"

"I just finished *A Tale of Two Cities* by Charles Dickens.

I read that to Mother when we were in Chicago."

"Dickens?" Kady said.

"Do you like Dickens?" Austin said.

"I don't know. I've never read any."

"That's all right," Austin said. "I didn't come here to read books anyway. I'm tired of reading."

"What did you come here for, then?" Kady said. "Charlotte and I would like to know."

Austin glanced over at his youngest cousin. She was sitting quietly on a corner of the blanket, red patent leather slippers sticking out from under her checkered dress. She was curling the scalloped bottom of her red apron around her finger. When he looked at her, she looked down at her lap.

"Charlotte!" Kady said suddenly. "It's the Patty Rollers!"

Charlotte glanced nervously behind her.

"You know what to do," Kady whispered to her.

Before Austin could even get a question out, Kady reached out and took him firmly under the chin.

"And you, Austin, you keep your mouth *closed.*"

Austin had to chomp down on his lips to keep them still. But when Kady let go of his chin and quickly flipped open her primer, he turned around to see who it was he was supposed to keep his mouth shut in front of. Patty Rollers, Kady had called them.

There were two men approaching on mangy-looking yellowish horses. Austin had to chomp down even harder to keep from crying out: *Baldy and Thin Beard! They dragged off that runaway slave at the train station.*

"Austin!" Kady hissed. "Turn around! And not a word— so help me!"

Austin scooted behind Charlotte. *If those men recognize*

me, he thought wildly, *they'll tell everyone I'm the abolitionist's son and I'm staying at the Ravenals'. Aunt Olivia will have Mother and Jefferson and me on a train before dinner!*

"Why don't you read first, Charlotte?" Kady said loudly.

"Oh, no," Austin said in an even louder voice. "Let me."

He snatched the book from Charlotte and propped it in front of his face. If he was reading, he'd have an excuse for keeping his face covered. Kady hesitated and her glance drifted over his shoulder again. Austin began to read.

"'A mouse that had seen very little of the world came running one day to his mother in great haste—'"

"Good mornin', there, Miz Ravenal!" a whiny voice called out.

Austin would have recognized it anywhere. That was Thin Beard all right, the one with the gun.

"'"Oh, Mother," said he,'" Austin read on, "'"I am frightened almost to death—"'"

Close by, the horses slowed to a stop and footsteps grew closer. Austin burrowed his face farther into the book.

"'"I have seen the strangest creature that ever was,"'" he read. "'"He has a fierce, angry look, and struts about on two legs—"'"

"I wouldn't let no child of mine read such things," a voice said. It came out like a low growl, and it made Austin want to shiver. It was like listening to a mad dog talk, just the way he remembered it.

"Well, he *isn't* any child of yours, Irvin Ullmann," Kady said primly. "Nor yours either, Barnabas Brown. Now please, what *is* it?"

"I'm sure you know what we're here about," whiny Barnabas said. "There's a slave missing. We're out to find him."

"I haven't seen any missing slaves," Kady said.

"Beggin' your pardon, Miz Ravenal," Irvin growled, "but your daddy's got upward of 200 slaves. You can tell every one of his from every one of Morris Singleton's?"

"Yes, I can," Kady said. Her voice was growing tighter.

"Then you haven't seen none of Morris Singleton's coloreds?" Barnabas said.

"No."

"How 'bout these chilrun?"

In front of him, Austin could feel Charlotte shaking her head. He clung to the sides of the book.

"How about that one there behind them covers?" Irvin snarled.

Austin held his breath.

"Well?"

Austin was suddenly aware of the smell of stale tobacco. "I haven't seen anything either!" he cried out from behind the book.

There was a suspicious silence. The tobacco odor grew closer.

"Who is that there anyway?" Irvin Ullmann barked.

Could they have recognized my voice? Austin thought frantically. And then it dawned on him. It was what they *didn't* hear that perked up their ears. He'd forgotten to use his southern drawl. He thrashed around in his mind for a way out. *How can I convince them I'm one of them so they'll go away?*

He pulled the book even closer to his nose. "I sure hope you find that miserable little cuffee!" he said in his best South Carolina accent.

"We'll catch him—and he'll pay!" Barnabas said.

"And then *we'll* get paid," Irvin added with a growl. "If you see any of Mr. Singleton's chattel where he ain't supposed to be, you let us know right quick."

"His name's Brawley," said Barnabas.

Austin listened to the crunch of their shoes across the grass. He didn't emerge until their horses' hooves pounded off down the road, and then he dropped the book into his lap in relief. "That was close!" he said. "Those men were at the train station when we arrived!"

"Is that so?" Kady said coldly.

Austin was stung. "Did I do something wrong?"

Kady just looked at him.

"Who were they?" Austin said. "What did you call them— Patty Rollers or something?"

"That's what the slaves call them," Kady said, her voice still frosty. "It comes from 'patrollers.' They spend all their time patrolling the area for slaves who are off their plantations without passes. They have to have written permission from their master or mistress to go off the land."

"What happens if the Patty Rollers catch them without one?" Austin said.

Kady's big eyes narrowed angrily. "The owners will pay the Patties a great deal of money for returning their property," she said. "Which the Patty Rollers do, after—"

"Don't say it, Kady, please!"

Austin looked at Charlotte in surprise. "Say what?"

"Charlotte, I believe it's your turn to read, honey," Kady said.

Then she pursed her lips at Austin. It was clear he wasn't to ask any more questions. And he had so many.

"Kady!" Charlotte whispered suddenly.

Austin saw that she was pointing toward the stand of trees. Austin didn't see anyone, but Charlotte apparently did. She got up on her knees and pointed even more excitedly.

"What?" Kady said.

"I think I saw him—one of Mr. Singleton's!"

"How could you tell that from here?" Austin whispered.

They both ignored him and, gathering up their skirts, dashed across the lawn toward the trees. Austin followed.

"You there—it's all right!" Kady called. "Just stop. We only want to talk to you!"

Kady's skirts slowed her down, and Austin caught up with her just as she reached the trees. Charlotte was already there, standing beside a very tall black man whose eyes were bulging from his head.

But when he saw Kady, the man's eyes relaxed.

"Brawley," Kady said, "you must be careful. The Patty Rollers were here very recently. Your master's discovered you are missing, and they're out looking for you."

Brawley's eyes lit with terror again.

"Now don't worry," Kady said. "You know you can hide here at Canaan Grove until nightfall. Charlotte, you show him a place. Make sure he gets there safe. And don't go to Seton's cabin. If they suspect, that's the first place they'll look."

Charlotte nodded and slipped her hand into Brawley's. He followed her off meekly through the trees. Austin started after her, but Kady caught at his sleeve.

"I think not, Austin," she said. "You come inside with me."

Then she snatched up her skirts again and walked hurriedly toward the house. Austin followed, running to keep up.

"Where will Brawley go when night comes?" he asked. "And why can't he go to Seton's cabin? Why would they look there first?"

Kady stopped in her tracks, and Austin nearly ran up the back of her skirt. She whirled to face him, her pretty face red and furious.

"If you want to learn about being a slave owner, Austin Hutchinson," she said stiffly, "you're going to have to ask someone else."

"I don't understand—" Austin stammered. He wanted to go on with his questions: *Why didn't you want the Patty Rollers to take Brawley back where he belonged? Why did you help him instead of the Patty Rollers? Don't you believe in slavery like your father?*

But Kady cut him off. "You're very smart—you'll figure it out. Lessons are over for today." She tossed her dark-brown hair with a jerk. "But don't you dare tell those Patty Rollers where Brawley is, do you hear me?" She swished away, hurling over her shoulder only one more sentence: "And if you tell anyone I told you that, I'll deny it, and you'll look like a liar!"

She was almost to the house when Austin shouted, "I would never do that!"

If she heard him, she didn't let on. She just disappeared inside. Austin followed, his spirits sinking like a lead weight.

No matter what I do, I turn somebody against me, he thought forlornly. *Pretty soon they'll all hate me!*

But not Uncle Drayton, he added in his mind. *He'll understand when I explain.*

When he walked in the front door, Aunt Olivia was rushing through the hall toward the dining room. "Dinner is ready," she said indignantly. "Where have you been? And where is Charlotte?"

He knew how to answer that one. "I don't know."

"Well, at least there's *something* you admit you don't know," she muttered. She fingered the sparkling purple brooch at her throat, and her eyes took on a suspicious glow. "Weren't you at lessons together?"

"Charlotte will be along in a moment," Kady said from the stairs, glaring at Austin. "I sent her on an errand."

"You know we eat dinner promptly at two," Aunt Olivia said fretfully. She gave Kady a second look and added, "You must slow down, Kady. A lady does not come down the stairs at a trot."

Charlotte rushed in, red-faced, from the back hall. Aunt Olivia clucked her tongue and led them all into the dining room. Out of the corner of his eye, Austin saw Charlotte nod to Kady. Kady gave her shoulder a squeeze that sent an ache of longing through Austin. It must feel good to be so close to someone.

"Now, then," Aunt Olivia said when they were all seated at the table and Tot and Mousie were, as always, hovering nearby. "Is it going well with the lessons?"

"Fine," Kady said. "But I don't think there is much I can teach Austin. He's read books I haven't even heard of."

"I'm sure there's *something* you know that I don't," Austin said to her.

"Thank you very much!" Kady said.

"I didn't mean—"

"Well, then," Aunt Olivia said briskly, passing the oysters, "there is only one thing to do."

Austin dared to hope that she meant to send him on to Charleston with Uncle Drayton, but she quickly dashed that.

"Austin," she said, "while Charlotte and Jefferson are at their lessons, you will go into your uncle's library and spend your time reading the books there."

Austin felt as if his lips were stuck. It was another disappointment—one he could barely cover.

"There are 200 volumes there," she went on. "I don't think even you could read them all in your time here."

Polly gave a shrill laugh, echoed by Tot. "I would think not. He isn't going to be here that long!"

"I suppose that would be fine," Austin said. What else could he say?

"Then that is settled," Aunt Olivia said. "You can begin tomorrow."

Austin didn't look at Kady. He knew she must be about to cheer. *And all I did was try to help,* he thought as he trailed his spoon through his soup.

"Kady, honey, two oysters are all a lady should eat at a sitting," Aunt Olivia said. "You don't want to look like a glutton."

Kady scooped two more from the platter. "Mama, I'm hungry and oysters are my favorite. No one can fix them like Josephine."

"Well, now, that's just fine," Aunt Olivia said with a little pout that showed it wasn't fine at all. "Just don't you come crying to me when your beaus complain because you eat like a field hand."

Austin's mind wandered listlessly from the conversation. He knew nothing about beaus or oysters or even field hands, and none of them seemed to care if he did or not.

I'm not one of them, he thought sadly. *I don't fit.*

✝ ✿ ✝

Chapter Nine

It started raining that night, and it rained for four days, turning all of Canaan Grove into a swamp no one could go out in. It seemed to turn *everyone* inside the plantation house into a sniveling whiner.

Aunt Olivia wailed that the weather would keep Uncle Drayton from returning on time. She feared she couldn't endure another day without him.

Polly said the damp weather took all the curl out of her hair, though Austin had never seen much there in the first place.

His mother coughed more than ever, although she said being able to lie in bed all the time and sleep as much as she wanted was just what she needed. At night, when Jefferson was asleep and it was their time together, Mother was usually already drowsy. There was no chance for the questions that still ran through his head when he climbed into bed.

Why don't the masters trust their slaves to go to other plantations? he wondered. *And what do the Patty Rollers do to them when they catch them?*

Which led him to another question. Polly had been so determined that he not tell anyone his father was an abolitionist—but Kady was mad when he pretended not to be.

Don't Kady and Charlotte believe in slavery like their father? Does Uncle Drayton know that? Should I tell him? If I tell Uncle Drayton, he will trust me and like me. But that isn't what Father would want me to do. And if I do, Kady and Charlotte will never be my friends. Not that they will anyway. I'm too different from them!

The only thing he knew for sure was that Charlotte seemed happier with Uncle Drayton being gone. She was certainly less nervous. Sometimes at the table, when Aunt Olivia was babbling away, Austin would catch Charlotte watching him from the other end of the table. He would smile at her, and she would smile back—a little.

Once he was coming down the stairs when she raced in the back door, soaked right down to her skin, hair plastered down on her head, and grinning. She didn't see him as she skipped through, looking very pleased with herself.

Seton had gone with Uncle Drayton, of course, and Austin missed him. Sometimes when he was supposed to be reading in the library, he curled up in the window seat and tried to think of ways to make it up to Seton for what had happened Sunday with the carriage. Some of the time he did read. He found some books about the history of South Carolina, and when he was tired of reading them, he dreamed he was one of King Charles II's explorers discovering Charles Towne—with friends.

By Saturday he was restless. He selected a skinny volume with the title *The Nat Turner Rebellion* and curled up in the window seat in the library and tried to concentrate. He was so lonely that he read out loud.

"'In 1831, a murdering slave named Nat Turner formed a group of some 60 slaves and led a rebellion. A patrol scattered Turner and his band in all directions but by this time, 55 whites had been killed.'"

Their master must not have treated them well the way Uncle Drayton treats his slaves, Austin thought. He gazed for a minute out the window and realized with a start that it had stopped raining. The sun was streaming into the library, and a figure was running past. It was Charlotte, her green-hooded shoulder cape flying out behind her. "You'd better run faster!" she squealed to someone. "I'll catch you!"

Charlotte, squealing? Austin thought. He craned his neck to see who she was chasing, but she was long gone.

There were three more figures out on the lawn, though. One belonged to Jefferson, zigzagging back and forth down the velvety steps toward the river. The other two were Polly and Tot, skirts pulled up nearly to their knees, hauling after him and screaming. The only person having fun there, Austin knew, was Jefferson.

Still, his little brother was with people who were paying attention to him. It was better than sitting in a stuffy library. The thing to do was to get away from the sight of the other children playing, he decided. Austin crawled under the desk and settled himself in.

"'The Nat Turner Rebellion and others like it,'" he read on, "'could have been avoided. Slave owners should beware of allowing their slaves to congregate without supervision for any reason. Even prayer meetings are to be viewed with suspicion—'"

"Step in here, young lady!" a voice commanded just outside the library door.

Austin sat up straight, banging his head on the underside

of the desk. Uncle Drayton was back!

The door came open and his uncle said, "Sit yourself down—right quick!"

The sharp edge on Uncle Drayton's voice told Austin now was not a good time to jump out and announce his presence.

"I thought I told you that you were not to associate with that boy!"

"You always let us play with the slave children."

Austin stifled a gasp. The "young lady" was Charlotte.

"Not that one!" Uncle Drayton said. "He was disrespectful to me last week, and I spoke to you about it. Then I left the plantation . . . and you deliberately disobeyed me. Didn't you?"

"Yes, sir."

"I might have let it pass, but just now—the minute I returned—he was insolent to me again, and I will not have it. You are not to so much as speak with him anymore."

"But, Daddy—"

"No more!"

It came out like a roar, and Austin found himself hugging his knees against his chest.

"Now, is that understood?"

"I understand," Charlotte said.

There was a short silence. "All right now, my sweet thing," Uncle Drayton said, sounding suddenly kind, "you run along and play. It's Saturday, after all. But you remember what I said."

Charlotte muttered something, and then there were two sets of footsteps and the sound of the door closing. Austin waited until he was sure they were gone before he slipped out.

There was a wind coming off the river that was scudding

the gray clouds away and drying up the soggy ground. Austin kept his head down as he walked, trying to avoid the puddles.

Charlotte is friends with one of the slave children, he thought. *Or at least she* was. *And now Uncle Drayton is telling her she can't be. I think I know how she must feel.*

Austin looked up to find himself on a road lined on both sides by the chimney ends of some wood-board houses, each with a porch and a roof made of cypress shingles. They seemed to go on endlessly down the street with only about 50 yards between them.

I wonder what these old buildings are, Austin thought. *It doesn't look like Uncle Drayton cares about them much— they all need painting.*

Still, there were some camellias blooming in front of a few of them, and almost every one had bright-colored curtains on the glassless windows. And from every chimney, there curled a thin wisp of smoke.

There wasn't anyone around to ask the questions that were popping in Austin's mind like corn—until at one cabin he saw a boy chopping at the ground in front of the small building with a bent hoe.

It was Henry-James, the boy who had saved Jefferson. Austin crossed the road and approached the fenced, square plot of dirt he was chopping at.

"Hello," Austin said, pushing open the gate.

The black boy's eyes looked as if they'd bulge from his box-shaped face. Beside him there came a low growling sound. Austin looked down to see a dog there with a big head as high as the boy's waist and enough skin on him for another bloodhound.

"You won't let him bite me, will you?" Austin said.

"Bite you? Bogie?" The black boy gave a hard laugh.

"What's so funny?" Austin said timidly.

"Bogie wouldn't bite nobody!" Henry-James said.

Austin looked doubtfully at the dog. He was still eyeing Austin from under the brown-furred skin that hung over his eyes and fell down over the rest of him in wrinkles. And he was still rumbling from down in his chest.

"He's growling at me," Austin said.

"No, he ain't. He's talkin' to you."

"What's he saying?" Austin said.

"He just askin' you who you are."

"Shall I tell him?" Austin said.

"I would."

"I'm Austin Hutchinson," he said to the dog. "I understand your name is Bogie."

In answer, the dog threw back its head and howled gleefully.

"Now what's he saying?" Austin said.

"He sayin' you ain't like the rest of the Ravenals."

"Oh," Austin said sadly. "He's right. I'm not like them at all—"

And then he stopped himself.

What if I tell him I am different? What if I tell him that I'm an abolitionist? He's sure to like me then. But then I'll be in trouble with Uncle Drayton and—I can't. I have to think of something else.

"Is he your dog?" Austin asked.

Henry-James nodded and went back to chopping at the ground.

"Where did you get him?"

"Marse Drayton," Henry-James said. "One of his prize

bloodhounds done had a litter of mutts. He was gonna drown them, and I begged him to let me keep one."

"You're lucky," Austin said. "I've never had a dog."

Henry-James sniffed. "Yeah, I's lucky all right."

It was quiet again, and Austin scrambled for something else to say. Bogie flopped back down. Henry-James kept hacking at the ground, though Austin was sure he saw him glance nervously over his shoulder at the wooden shack.

Austin looked curiously at the square plot of dirt. "Isn't this a little small for a plantation garden? How many people could this possibly feed?"

Henry-James's black eyes flicked up to Austin's face. "Ain't no plantation garden," he said. "This feed my mama and my grandpappy and me."

"This is *your* garden?" Austin said.

"Yessir," Henry-James said gruffly. "And that there's my house."

He pointed to the cabin and went back to digging. Austin looked again at the tiny cabin. Even as he stared, one of the curtains moved and something green disappeared behind them.

"Was that your mama looking out just then?" Austin asked.

Henry-James looked sharply at the cabin. "No," he said in a curt voice. "My mama's down at the nursin' cabin bindin' up somebody's busted leg. You imaginin' things."

Austin nodded solemnly. "I do sometimes." He frowned back at the window. The curtain wavered again, and a small, white hand yanked back out of sight.

"I'm not dreaming *this* up, though," Austin said insistently. "I think there's a white person in your house."

Henry-James whipped around to look at the window, the

hoe falling out of his hand and barely missing Bogie's head. Austin was sure he saw fear dancing in the slave's eyes.

"What's wrong?" Austin said. "Isn't whoever that is supposed to be in there?"

"Ain't nobody in there," Henry-James said. He turned quickly and picked up his hoe, pounding it savagely at the ground. "Beggin' your pardon, Massa Austin, but Slave Street ain't no place for you. Why don't you go on back up to the Big House?"

"But I really did see—"

"It ain't your business—"

And then the shack door opened, and a deer-colored head poked out.

"Charlotte!" Austin said.

His cousin slipped out the door, pulling her bright-green cape around her. Austin stared from her to Henry-James and back again. The black boy leaned on his hoe and glared at the ground.

"I don't think he'll tell anybody, Henry-James," Charlotte said. She looked at Henry-James as if she were waiting for him to give her permission to say more.

"You don't have to worry about me," Austin said glumly. "Even if I told somebody whatever it is, they wouldn't listen to me anyway."

Henry-James grunted and went back to his chopping. That was obviously the go-ahead Charlotte needed, because she shrugged in Austin's direction and said, "Thank you."

She sank down on the middle step. Austin edged toward her.

"So, you're doing it anyway," he said. "I heard your father. I was under the desk. I wasn't hiding or eavesdropping or anything," he added hurriedly. "That's just where I like to read, but what I meant was, you're seeing Henry-James even though your father told you not to."

"And I told her she better get on home," Henry-James said. He was strangling the hoe handle. "Her daddy likely to be along any minute lookin' for me. She don't need him findin' her here."

"When we saw you coming just now, we thought Daddy had sent you to fetch him," Charlotte said. "That's why I hid inside."

Henry-James watched Austin so intently that Bogie gathered his wrinkled self up from the ground and came over to Austin to sniff suspiciously at his pant leg.

This is my last chance, Austin thought in agony. *If Henry-James sends me packing, Charlotte will never speak to me again, that's for sure. She'll do anything he says, anybody could see that. I wish somebody felt like that about me.*

"I just have a feeling he's telling the truth," Charlotte said. She looked shyly at Austin. "You won't tell Daddy, will you?"

"If Uncle Drayton had sent me out here for that," Austin said, "I wouldn't have done it."

"You lyin', boy," Henry-James said. "That ain't true at all."

"It is!" Austin blurted out. "My father is an abolitionist. We don't believe in slavery!"

There. He'd said it. He looked anxiously at Charlotte.

She was tilting her chin up at Henry-James. "See, I told you," she said.

"But you told me he called Brawley a 'miserable little cuffee,' too."

"I was trying to help!" Austin said.

"So that there was a lie," Henry-James said, drilling his black eyes into Austin.

"The whole thing was a lie! We were trying to protect that slave!"

Charlotte shook her finger at Henry-James. "I *told* you, and I tried to tell Kady, too." She looked at Austin. "Nobody listens to me either."

"I promise you," Austin said, "I will never tell Uncle Drayton I saw you out here."

"Well, she ain't comin' back here no more anyways," Henry-James said angrily. He tossed the hoe aside and kicked at the dirt.

"Why not?" Austin said.

"Because!" Charlotte said. "You heard it yourself—Daddy said no."

"Why?"

"'Cause I answer Marse Drayton back today."

"Why?"

"Don't you never stop askin' questions?" Henry-James said.

But his face wasn't so tight as he stalked over to the porch and plopped down on the bottom step.

"I guess I don't," Austin said. He settled on the top step. No one chased him off.

"We only s'pose to work until noon on Saturday," Henry-James said. "I told Daddy Elias to come on with me—"

"Who's Daddy Elias?" Austin said.

"His grandfather," Charlotte said.

"I told Daddy Elias we'd have us some cornbread and molasses for dinner. Marse Drayton come by and say since

Daddy Elias an overseer, he got to see to those darkies fixin'
that dike down to the south, and I say, 'Marse Drayton, Daddy
Elias got to *eat*—he too old to be workin' without no food.'"

"He's the one you were taking those biscuits for!" Austin
said. "Well, you were just standing up for your grandfather."

"But the slaves aren't supposed to talk back to my father,"
Charlotte said. "They're just supposed to do what he tells
them."

"And you are, too," Austin said.

She nodded sadly. "Most of the time I don't mind so
much . . . but Henry-James is the only friend I have!"

Austin looked from one of them to the other. *If I had one,*
he thought, *I'd do anything to keep him.*

"You have to keep playing together!" he burst out.

Henry-James gave a grunt. "I gots to keep my teeth in my
mouth. Marse Drayton knock them right out of my head if he
find out I'm still runnin' 'round here with Miss Lottie."

"Only if he found out," Austin said.

"Ain't no way Marse Drayton won't find out," Henry-
James said.

"He's right," Charlotte said. "What if we got so involved
in a game we forgot to be careful?"

"That wouldn't happen if you had help," Austin said.

Charlotte rolled her eyes. "Who would help us? They'd
say we were silly!"

"I wouldn't."

Henry-James and Charlotte both looked at Austin, and
Henry-James picked thoughtfully at the space between his
two front teeth.

"You'd help us?" he said.

"Yes!" Austin said.

"How we know we can trust you?" Henry-James said.

He stared hard at Austin, and even Bogie sat up and looked at him from under the skin hanging over his eyes.

"If I'm playing *with* you," Austin said slowly, "then it's as much my secret as it is yours. Why would I want Uncle Drayton to find out and punish *me?*"

After a moment, Henry-James cautiously nodded his closely cropped woolen head. "But soon's I find out Marse Drayton suspect anything, you both go on back up to the Big House to *stay,*" he said.

"I promise," Charlotte said.

"Me, too!" Austin said. He could barely hold himself back from trying a handspring across the garden.

"Uh-oh," Henry-James said. Bogie sat upright and pulled his long, droopy ears back from his face.

"Here come my mama up the road," he said. He looked sternly at Austin and Charlotte. "Now, ain't nobody gonna tell her that Marse Drayton say we can't play no more. She don't like sneakin' around."

"Not a word," Austin said. "My lips are sealed with sealing wax."

"Mine, too," Charlotte said.

"Then I reckon there gonna be trouble 'round these here parts," said a voice behind them.

Austin looked up to the doorway. The oldest person he'd ever seen was standing there shaking a very white head.

"Mmmm-mmmm," the old man said. "There gonna be *real* trouble."

✝-✞-✝

ustin saw that Henry-James wouldn't look up.

"Yessir," the old man said. "Whenever chilrun start to sealin' they mouths, there gonna be big trouble."

No one seemed to be able to say a word. It was clear to Austin that he was going to have to take charge or their whole game was over. He stood up and stuck out his hand.

"Hello, sir," he said to the man. "I'm Austin Hutchinson. I just want you to know, I'm going to make sure there won't be any trouble."

The old man put out a dark hand and clasped Austin's in it. It felt like a piece of hardened leather against Austin's palm.

"You Marse Drayton's kin," he said. His voice was hoarse, like he'd used it for so long that it was about to wear out. Austin could even hear his breath whistling through his nose as if it, too, were working on rusty parts.

"I'm his nephew," Austin said.

The old man's soft eyelids crinkled around a pair of tiny, clouded eyes. "That gonna be a trick, sure 'nuff. What you young'uns sealin' your lips about?"

Austin tried to hold back a sigh of relief. The old man hadn't heard their whole conversation—*that* was a good thing.

But Henry-James still hadn't looked up, and Charlotte was rolling the edge of her apron around her finger until it was turning blue at the tip. Austin smiled to himself. These two needed him more than he'd suspected.

"You haven't told me *your* name," Austin said.

The old man smiled, his lower lip curving out like a spoon. "Elias Ravenal," he said politely. "They calls me Daddy Elias most of the time."

"Is that because you're the oldest?" Austin said.

"It's 'cause he the most important!" Henry-James said. He let his eyes flicker up and then back to the porch floor.

"What makes you so important?" Austin said.

Daddy Elias bobbed his head as if he were embarrassed.

"Whenever anybody on the Street has a worry or a trouble, they always come to Daddy Elias," Charlotte said. "He can make almost anything bad go away, just by talking about it."

Austin felt his eyes getting big. "You *can?*" he said. "Do you have some kind of magic power?"

Daddy Elias chuckled deep in his throat. "Ain't no magic power," he said. "I just knows my Jesus."

"You do?" Austin said. "I never really thought about Him much—"

"Never thought 'bout *Jesus?*" Henry-James cried.

"Henry-James Ravenal!" A tall woman with a checkered cloth wrapped around her hair was opening the gate with long, slender fingers and directing her stern eyes at Henry-James. "Don't you be talkin' to nobody like that—'specially

Marse Drayton's kinfolk."

"That's all right," Austin said. "Everybody talks to me like that."

Her eyes landed on Austin. "No, it ain't all right—'scuse me for sayin'. Henry-James know his manners."

"Sorry," Henry-James mumbled.

The tall woman, whom Austin assumed was Henry-James's mother, picked her way past them up the steps.

"Hello, Miss Lottie," she said to Charlotte.

"Hello, Ria," Charlotte said. "I was just telling my cousin how much store everybody sets by what Daddy Elias says."

"It's just Jesus talkin' through him, is all," Ria said. She didn't smile, but her face looked smooth with pride. She *was* like Henry-James, Austin decided. Everybody listened to them.

There was a shout from the end of Slave Street.

"Glory in my soul!" a chorus of voices called out.

Ria leaned out over the railing, and Henry-James sprang up.

"Glory in my soul!" they both shouted back—half calling, half singing. Daddy Elias's voice crackled out an "Amen!"

Austin watched as a bevy of women in ragged aprons and bright-colored head scarves moved down the street, clapping their hands and singing out again, "Glory in my soul!" They surrounded a tall, broad-shouldered black man.

"Seton!" Austin cried.

But Austin's voice was lost in the singing. Above it all, Seton's voice rang out into the wintry air. It sounded just like the voice Austin had heard that Sunday when he'd been sitting by the pond.

"Oh, I takes my text in Matthew—and some in Revelation!" Seton sang.

"Glory to my soul, Lord!" everyone answered back. "Glory to my soul!"

"Oh, I knows you by your love for Him—there's a meetin' here tonight."

"Glory to my soul, Lord—" the street singers replied.

But Ria brushed her hands briskly on her apron and turned to Charlotte. "You gonna have to 'scuse us, Miss Lottie," she said. "We got business to tend to."

"I know," Charlotte said. "Come on, Austin."

Henry-James and his mother and grandfather hurried into their house, and Charlotte led Austin out the gate and away from Slave Street with the singing fading off behind them.

"Why did we have to leave?" Austin said.

"That song," Charlotte said. "That was a message to all the slaves that there's going to be a meeting tonight. Seton does it now that Daddy Elias is so old his voice doesn't work very well."

"Why doesn't he just tell them?"

Charlotte lowered her voice. "Because they aren't allowed to have meetings."

"Oh, I know why," Austin said. "Your father is afraid they'll plan a rebellion or something."

"I don't know. It's just part of the Slave Code."

"But I don't understand," Austin said. "If your father owns the slaves, why do you and Kady help them when they try to—"

Charlotte stopped suddenly. They had just emerged from the trees. Beyond them was the long brick building Seton had gone into last Sunday. Even from here it had the pungent smell of leather and horses' sweat.

"You've never ridden a horse, have you?" she said.

Austin felt his heart stop. "No," he said.

She gave his arm a yank. "Come on, then!"

It turned out that the brick building was the stable. Isaac—the slave with arms big as fireplace logs who had helped Seton save his father from drowning—was the stable-hand. He told Charlotte that, yes, indeed, missie, they could take a ride on Zelda. Then, of course, Austin's questions began.

"Which one is Zelda? Is that a mare or a gelding? She's sorrel-colored, right? How do I keep her from stopping and throwing me off? I don't want the same trouble I had with the carriage."

"So that's what happened in the carriage that day," Charlotte said as Isaac set about saddling the horse. "Seton let you drive."

"I didn't mean for Seton to get in trouble!"

Charlotte shook her silky head. "Seton wouldn't have done it if he didn't like you. If it had been Polly, he'd have told Daddy about it and then some!"

"Really?" Austin said.

Charlotte shrugged it off. "Zelda is a mare and she's getting pretty old, so you shouldn't have any trouble. Besides, I'll be on her right behind you so nothing will go wrong."

Zelda took them everywhere Austin had wanted to go since he'd been at Canaan Grove. With the leather creaking pleasantly under them and Charlotte giving Austin directions from behind, they rode through the barnyard and the pasture.

Austin was sorry to leave the animals behind, until Zelda took them past the windmill and the sugar cane mill.

"If you're still here in the fall," Charlotte said, "you can watch the slaves take the juice out of the cane and boil it into molasses."

"Is that where molasses comes from?" Austin said.

Charlotte just laughed—but Austin didn't feel like she was laughing at him.

There was so much to see, Austin thought his neck might snap from all the twisting back and forth. Charlotte showed him the barns where the rice was threshed and stored, and the blacksmith's shop and the carpenters' building. There were places for potters and spinners and weavers and laundresses and even milliners, who made all the hats. He finally found out that the gurgling building by the pond was the spring house for storing food and milk.

"Canaan Grove is like a town!" Austin exclaimed.

"And that isn't all of it," Charlotte said. "There're also a thousand acres of rice fields, plus the gardens and the swamps—"

"Swamps?" Austin said. "Like the ones we passed going to church?"

"Yes."

"I've never been to one! Let's go see."

Austin felt her poke her heels into Zelda's sides, and they were off.

It grew chillier as Zelda pounded her hooves along a muddied sand path away from the barnyard and its buildings, but Austin felt a warm glow.

"Let's go faster, Charlotte!" he cried.

And they did, until Austin's seat came up out of the saddle and the air burned cold on his face. As soon as the swamp came into sight, however, slowing down was the only thing to do. There was something deliciously spooky about it that made going fast seem wrong somehow. Austin gave a delighted shiver.

The trees creaked as they rubbed together. Acorns popped under Zelda's hooves. Overhead, a single crow gave a sudden, raucous caw that made Austin jump in the saddle.

"Did that scare you?" Charlotte whispered.

"Yes," Austin whispered back—because it seemed only right to talk in a low voice. "I love it!"

"I never knew anyone else who liked the swamps," Charlotte said.

"A person could have adventures here."

She was quiet for a second. "Excuse me for saying this," she said, "but you like to have adventures? I thought you only liked to read and be smart."

"I only do that because that's all anyone will *let* me do," Austin said. He looked at her suddenly. "Just like I thought you were quiet and shy."

She shook her head. "I'm only quiet when nobody wants to hear what I have to say."

"I guess everybody wishes I would learn to do that," Austin said.

"So what kinds of adventures have you had?"

"I've never had one," he said matter-of-factly. "I thought I would have some when I came here, but even the slaves have more excitement than I do. They're having a secret meeting right now! I'd give anything to go to a secret meeting that was called by people singing a mystery code!" He twisted in the saddle to look at her again. "Do they meet in the swamps?"

"No," Charlotte said. "They don't come near them 'cause of how many of them have got sick here. The only people more frightened of the swamps are the Patty Rollers. They think the ghosts of all the dead slaves they once turned in come back to the swamps and wait to haunt them."

"You don't believe that, do you?" Austin said.

"Of course not. Daddy Elias says it isn't Christian to believe in ghosts."

"If nobody else uses the swamp for a meeting place, this would be the perfect place for us . . . well, for you and Henry-James to play."

Charlotte looked doubtfully around her. "I don't think Henry-James would come here. But there are plenty of other places."

"All right, we could have adventures anywhere! And I could find some way to signal you that the way was clear—and I'd keep watch."

"It's true—you *could* climb a tree," Charlotte said thoughtfully. "Henry-James could teach you bird calls."

Austin laughed out loud, and the sound echoed with wonderful creepiness over the marsh. "That's perfect!" he cried. "And I could—"

But Charlotte gave a sharp *"Shhh!"*

"What?" Austin hissed.

She pointed to the opposite bank of the swamp.

Austin followed with his eyes—just in time to see something white disappear beyond the cypress trees.

"What was that?" he whispered.

Behind him, he felt Charlotte shudder. "I don't know, but I think there's someone there."

✝ ⚜ ✝

Chapter Eleven

"**L**et's chase him!" Austin whispered hoarsely.

But Charlotte shook her head and took the reins into her own hands from behind Austin, turning Zelda back from the swamp.

"With it getting dark and all, you don't go chasing strangers through the swamps."

Austin actually liked the thought, but he decided not to push his luck.

It had been a lucky day anyway, he decided later as he lay in bed with Jefferson squirming in his sleep beside him. And there was the glimmer of a hope that he was going to spend *more* time with Henry-James and Charlotte.

All right, he told himself. *They might never like me as much as they like each other. But I don't think they hate me like Aunt Olivia and Polly do.*

That was enough to send him peacefully off to sleep.

When he woke up, it was still gray at the window, and for a few minutes he couldn't figure out why his eyes had suddenly come open. Then he heard it from across the hall—a deep sound, like rocks being stirred in a bucket. It was his mother coughing again. Austin slipped out of bed and went to her.

She struggled to sit up. "It's all right, Austin," she said.

"Should I fetch Aunt Olivia?"

"No!" She patted the bed, and Austin slipped in beside her. She wrapped both arms around him, and slowly she started to breathe easily.

"Let's talk for a minute," she said. "That helps. Tell me what you've been doing. I've barely seen you all week."

Austin snuggled in beside her and opened his mouth to start spinning out his story. But just as quickly he shut it.

I can't tell her! This has to be a secret from everybody else.

Austin squirmed a little. If he couldn't tell his mother—the one person he told everything to—was this the right thing to do?

"Austin, are you all right?" his mother asked.

"I'm just tired," he said.

She nodded into the pillows. "You sleep then," she said. And in a few minutes, her breathing was soft and even. Then his questions crowded in.

Is that the right thing—covering up Charlotte and Henry-James's friendship so I can have one, too?

Maybe I'll have to lie to Uncle Drayton. And maybe Mother, too.

But what if I didn't help them? What then?

Loneliness suddenly filled the room, and Austin shook his head in the dark.

I've made a decision and I'm going to stick to it, he thought firmly.

Austin was thinking so hard about that that he almost

missed the Bible story in church again the next day. But as soon as the singing and clapping finished ringing through the rafters, Austin listened. The man Jesus—they'd all been talking about Him yesterday. Austin wanted to be able to join in the conversation.

This week, the man Jesus was pulling children up onto His lap, and at first that didn't impress Austin. But then Reverend Pullens said, "And do you know what those people said to our Lord Jesus when those sweet chilrun crowded around Him, brothers and sisters?"

There was a general muttering of nos and disapproving grunts from the gallery.

"He said, 'You let those chilrun come to Me! Let them get right up here on My lap! They're the ones I want to see—they're the important ones!'"

All the slaves nodded their heads in agreement. Austin looked to see if Aunt Olivia and Uncle Drayton were nodding, too.

Uncle Drayton was—in the midst of a catnap. Aunt Olivia was busy adjusting the ribbon on Polly's skirt.

"Austin!" Jefferson hissed loudly.

Austin leaned down impatiently. *"What?"*

"I have to use the necessary!"

Austin glanced down the pew. Polly was already glaring at him.

"Can't you wait?" Austin said, barely moving his mouth.

"No!" Jefferson whispered. His voice got louder. "I'll wet my pants!"

Austin felt his face going crimson. He didn't even look back down the pew, where he could hear the silk rustling angrily.

He never did get to hear the rest of the story.

Later, as he was climbing up into the driver's seat, Austin heard Polly wailing to her mother from inside the carriage.

"They talk about going to the necessary—in *church!* Mama, our *darkies* have more sense than they do!"

"I've spoken to your father about it," Aunt Olivia said.

Austin's face burned, but he felt a tap on his shoulder and he looked up.

"Don't you pay them no mind," Seton said softly. "You got friends you don't even know 'bout yet."

That was all it took to make Austin's heart do some singing and clapping of its own. And after dinner, something happened to make it nearly pop out of his chest with joy— and he knew he'd made the right choice.

He was leaving the dining room when Charlotte put her mouth close to his ear. Polly was putting up a fuss about something, so no one else heard Charlotte say, "Henry-James says to meet him at the pond soon as you can."

Austin changed his clothes like a madman and ran out to find Henry-James sitting at the edge of the pond with his fishing pole, with Bogie stretched out in the early February sun beside him. He opened one eye and slapped his tail on the grass.

"I got here soon as I could," Austin said breathlessly.

"And you made enough noise doin' it," Henry-James said.

"I know. I'm going to have to work on being sneakier. Especially if I'm going to keep away from Jefferson."

"That your little brother?" Henry-James said.

"Yes. I suppose I should thank you for saving him from drowning the day we got here. At the moment I'm not very grateful."

"I didn't do nothin'," Henry-James said. "He was already

out of the water and plowin' 'cross the yard when he practically run right into me. I just picked him up and carried him back." He bobbed his pole in the water.

Austin tried not to fidget. "Charlotte said you wanted to see me," he said.

"That's right," Henry-James said. He pulled a wriggling, silvery fish out of the water. "You really gonna help Miss Lottie and me?"

"Of course!" Austin said. "We can have our own secret meetings, just like you and the other slaves do—"

Henry-James looked at him sharply. "She done tol' you 'bout those?" the black boy asked.

"Well . . . yes," Austin said. "But you don't have to worry! I'm not going to tell anyone. You can trust me."

Henry-James only grunted.

Austin nervously licked his lips. "So, what about tomorrow?"

"After the folks goes back to work after dinner," Henry-James said. He pointed across the pond to a wooded area thick with oaks and poplars. "Just beyond them trees."

"Perfect," Austin said. "There's a branch that hangs out over the water. I can sit up there and be the lookout. Now, I'll—"

"First thing you gonna have to do is hush that mouth," Henry-James said. "You make more noise than a mockingbird."

"I'll work on that, too," Austin whispered.

"Can you get the word to Miss Lottie without tellin' everybody in St. Paul's Parish?"

Austin just nodded—and smiled. There wasn't a doubt in his mind anymore.

He spent most of the night forming plans and then

tossing them out. There were plenty of *easy* ways to tell Charlotte where they were meeting Henry-James the next day, but none of them sounded adventurous. Finally, it all came together like a puzzle, with only one missing piece, and he could find that tomorrow, right in Uncle Drayton's library.

But for a few anxious moments the next morning, it didn't look as if that were going to work out at all. After breakfast when Polly and Tot came dragging their feet to Mother's room to fetch Jefferson for lessons, he took one look at Polly and let out a scream that curdled Austin's blood.

"*Noooo!*" he shrieked. "I don't want to go with *her!*"

Mother started to say something to him, but she went into such a fit of coughing, she could only wave her hand at Austin. He grabbed Jefferson by the collar and dragged him out into the hall.

"What's the matter?" he said to his little brother.

"I want to be with you! We always used to play!"

"No!" Austin said. *You'll spoil everything!*

Jefferson at once opened his mouth to scream, and Austin muffled it with both hands. Through the bedroom door, he could hear Polly whining.

"Those boys have ruined everything," she said. "I wish they would just—disappear!"

Austin's brain came to life like a lamp with a new wick. "You can have more fun with Polly than with me," he said.

He pulled his hands away from Jefferson's mouth, and the little boy puckered his tiny black brows. "She wants me to disappear."

"So do it. Go with her—then run away and hide—and make her spend the whole day looking for you."

Jefferson's face dimpled into a devilish grin.

"I knew you'd like that idea," Austin said.

I'll have to think of something else for tomorrow, he thought as he pushed Jefferson into the room and made for the library.

By the time the bell rang from the dining room for dinner, Austin was ready. As soon as the chicken pie and greens were served, Austin cleared his throat and said, "I read some poetry in the library this morning."

"How nice," Aunt Olivia said without interest. "Drayton, have some apple butter on your biscuits?"

"I'd like to recite some of it for you," Austin said.

"I'm glad to hear you're making good use of your time in my library, Austin," Uncle Drayton said quickly. "Why don't we hear what everyone else studied this morning?"

"You know, Father," Kady said, "I think I'd like to hear Austin recite some poetry."

Austin was almost too surprised to speak. But Charlotte was looking at him curiously from down the table. He cleared his throat.

"'As I went over the pond,'" he said, "'the pond went under me. I saw two little blackbirds sitting on a tree. The one called me rascal. The other called me thief. I took my little black stick, and knocked out all their teeth!'"

"Oh!" Polly cried. "You wretched boy! Mama!"

Aunt Olivia pulled her napkin away from her astounded mouth and looked at her husband. "Drayton!" she wailed.

"Now, Austin," Uncle Drayton said, twitching his neck inside his cravat, "couldn't you have chosen something more appropriate for the dinner table?"

"I found it in your library, sir," Austin said.

"Oh," Uncle Drayton said. He turned abruptly to Charlotte. "Suppose you tell us what *you* learned today, my sweet thing?"

"Nothing so entertaining as that, I can tell you," Kady said.

Austin looked up at her in surprise. Her soft, honey-colored eyes twinkled at him for a second, and then she went back to her chicken pie. Austin darted his glance to Charlotte. She looked directly at her mother and said, "Mama, I was so interested in what Kady and I were reading this morning that I think I'll take my book to that tree that hangs over the pond and read there instead of resting in my room after dinner."

Aunt Olivia threw up her hands. "I suppose I ought to give up any hopes of turning you into a lady if you're going to insist on being just like Kady."

"Thank you, Mama," Kady said dryly.

Uncle Drayton set about smoothing that over, and Polly set about taking sides with her mother. Charlotte ignored them all and looked across the table at Austin. He felt his face easing into a slow grin as he nodded at her. She grinned back, and she nodded, too.

✝ ✚ ✝

Chapter Twelve

f I dreamed it a thousand different ways, Austin said to himself, *I could never make a day better than this.*

He looked down from the thick branch of the oak he was perched on and once more made sure that Charlotte and Henry-James—and Bogie—were safe from the eyes of the world. They'd just finished a game of Blind Man's Buff.

Henry-James was now leaning against the tree with Bogie's head in his lap, calling out a chant while Charlotte jumped rope.

"Chickama, Chickama, Craney-Crow, went to the well to wash my toe! When I got back, my chicken was gone! Packed her things and went to town! Chickama, Chickama, now you're out! Chickama, Chickama, don't you pout!"

Charlotte squealed out her laugh, and Austin scanned the plantation to be sure no one had heard her.

"The coast is still clear!" he hissed down to them.

Henry-James rolled his big eyes up. "For somebody so smart, you got a powerful weak memory."

"What did I forget?" Austin whispered.

"The signal I done taught you."

"You taught me the whippoorwill signal for somebody coming. You didn't give me one for nobody coming."

"Then you don't got to say nothin'."

"Oh," Austin said.

He resituated himself on the limb so he could look behind him at Slave Street. All was quiet there except for the black children who were playing a game with a stick outside one cabin with a bent-over black woman watching over them. Henry-James had explained—when Austin had asked, of course—that the slave children didn't work until they were 13, except to do small jobs and help their own families. Everyone else was off doing their jobs, and the world belonged to the three of them.

Well, maybe the two of them, Austin thought. He could hear Charlotte and Henry-James whispering below. He couldn't help wishing he was in on their secret.

"Austin!" Charlotte called up to him.

He jumped. "What's wrong? Did you hear something?"

"Why don't you come down and play with us?"

"But what about your lookout?" Austin said.

"Just for a minute," Charlotte said. "It won't hurt."

Austin came off the tree with a tumble onto the still-soggy ground, and Bogie came over and sniffed at him. Henry-James shook his head.

"How you get to be 'leven years old and you ain't never climbed a tree?"

"I've just been in cities," Austin said.

"What kinda games you play in them cities?" Henry-James said.

"Marbles and checkers and chess, mostly," Austin said. "Sometimes jacks. You can play those on trains and in the backs of lecture halls without disturbing anybody."

"You didn't play hide the switch or fox and geese?" Charlotte said.

Austin shook his head. He'd never even heard of those games.

"How 'bout mumblety-peg?" Henry-James said.

"What's that?"

"That's where you throws a knife in the ground to make it stick. Person loses got to pull it out with his teeth."

"That's an awful game!" Charlotte said. "I don't play that either!"

"I would try it, though," Austin said.

Henry-James looked at him doubtfully. "You ever held a knife?"

"No," Austin said.

"Then we better be thinkin' of somethin' else."

And fast, Austin thought, *or I'll be sent back up the tree. I've waited and dreamed about this for so long—*

Then why not make it come true?

"There are some games I've *wanted* to play," he said slowly. "Things I've thought up and read about."

Henry-James frowned, but Charlotte said, "Like what?"

"Like pretending we're the first people to land in Charles Towne—the way they did back in 1670."

"I don't know nothin' 'bout that," Henry-James said.

"I bet *you* do, though, don't you?" Charlotte said to Austin.

"I know *some,*" Austin said modestly.

"I think that mean we gonna be here a while," Henry-James said.

"Good!" Charlotte said. "Go on, Austin. Tell us what to do."

As it turned out, he didn't have to do much telling. As soon as Austin said that the settlers from England had a hard time getting to Carolina because of storms at sea, Charlotte cried, "Let's start there!" and Henry-James said, with a little less enthusiasm, "We could sit in that there ol' broken boat down by the rice mill."

Austin felt as if he were still in his dream as the three of them crept in and out of the bushes all along the rice mill pond to the mill with Bogie scouting the way.

Next to the rice mill there was a cove in the river shielded from the rest of the plantation by an overgrowth of bamboo. A canoe-shaped boat with a split bottom had been pulled up onto the bank and seemed to be just waiting for dry-land passengers.

"We'll pretend it's a big English ship," Austin said. He bowed to Henry-James. "And you'll be the captain."

Henry-James blinked at him for a moment, and then the hint of a smile crossed his lips. He stepped into the dugout.

For hours they played—sailing the turbulent waves of the Atlantic Ocean and nearly losing Mistress Charlotte to its treacherous waters until she was rescued by the brave Sir Henry-James and the crafty Lord Austin and the strong-toothed Baron Von Bogie. Sir Henry-James pretended to be seasick over the side, until Mistress Charlotte told him that was disgusting, and Lord Austin harpooned every kind of attacking sea creature with his bamboo spear, with Baron Von Bogie retrieving it every time.

Austin was standing up on the bow when he saw the imaginary coast of South Carolina coming into view.

"Land!" he cried.

But Henry-James yanked him down by the seat of his pantaloons and sprayed a *Shhh!* onto the back of his neck. Bogie was whining and snuffling at the edge of the bamboo. There was a rustling sound on the other side.

Henry-James peered through, Bogie nudging to get his snout in beside him. The underbrush crackled again—*as if someone were trying to sneak up on us,* Austin thought with a chill.

"Can you see anybody?" he hissed close to Henry-James's ear.

The air was suddenly pierced with a voice like a nail being scraped down the side of a water glass.

"Jeffer-son! Where you is?"

"It's Tot!" Charlotte whispered frantically.

Austin's eyes met her wild ones. "They're looking for Jefferson!"

"And we done foun' him," Henry-James said. He pointed to Bogie, who had his head stuck through two stalks of bamboo, tail wagging—*with a purpose,* Austin thought.

Henry-James stood up, stepped off the dugout, and reached between the bamboo. He came back with a wriggling bundle of arms and legs in a puffed-sleeve tunic and knee pants. Somewhere in there wagged a tousled head of dark hair.

"Let me go, you cuffee!" the figure shrieked.

Henry-James planted a hand over Jefferson's mouth and held him so tight that his blue eyes began to bulge.

"He won't let you go unless you promise to stop screaming," Charlotte whispered to him.

Jefferson managed to nod. Austin had to smile to himself. He was sure he'd never seen Jefferson look that terrified.

"*And* until you promise never to call him a cuffee again," Charlotte said. "He's a person—good as you."

Austin looked at her. There it was again. She sounded just like his mother and father—

Henry-James slowly pulled his hand away. "I'm gonna put you down now," he whispered. "But don't you try runnin' off, you hear?"

Jefferson shook his head as his high-topped shoes hit the bank. "I don't want to run off," he whispered. "I want to play with you all."

Austin groaned. "You're supposed to be with Polly and Tot, shrimp."

"But you told me to run away from them," Jefferson said.

Henry-James and Charlotte looked at Austin.

"I did tell him that," Austin said sheepishly. "I had to because . . . it's a long story."

Henry-James peeked through the bamboo. "It gonna be a short story if them girls finds us."

There was another blood-chilling screech from Tot.

"Polly will run straight to Mama," Charlotte said.

"Why?" Jefferson said.

"Hush up, shrimp," Austin said.

"No!" Jefferson said. "Is this a secret? Is that why you're all hiding in there?"

"I'm telling you, if we throw him back out there to Polly, he's going to tell everybody on the plantation," Austin said.

"Jefferson!" someone else shouted. "You little brat—I'm going to skin you when I find you!"

"Polly!" Charlotte whispered.

Henry-James looked through the bamboo once more. "I know where to go—but you all got to do just as I say."

Austin poked Jefferson. "You hear that, shrimp?" he whispered.

Jefferson pulled away from him and edged close to Henry-James. As Austin watched in amazement, he slipped his chubby hand into the black boy's. Henry-James hauled Jefferson up onto his back and said, "Follow me."

They did—once again with Bogie leading the way with his quivering nose—away from the direction of the house, through thick woods and along a narrow strip of marshy ground between the big rice mill pond and another small swamp. Austin kept his eyes fastened to Henry-James's head and Bogie's tail. By the time they reached Slave Street, they couldn't even hear Polly and Tot anymore.

Henry-James dumped Jefferson off his back in front of his cabin and opened the gate.

"Whose house is this?" Jefferson said as he followed them into the yard. "Are we going inside? Is this my hiding place?"

Henry-James looked at Austin. "He ask more questions than you do!"

Inside, the whole house was the size of Uncle Drayton's dining room—just two rooms, one behind the other, divided by the fireplace with its big iron cooking pot.

The front room appeared to be their "parlor" with a wood floor whose cracks were filled with hard mud. There wasn't any glass on the two windows—just the faded red curtains and some shutters, which must have made it very dark when they were closed.

It was dim even with the fading afternoon light filtering through, but Austin could still see the plank table and two benches under one window. There was a sideboard in the corner with an odd collection of cracked crockery and glasses. Next to the fireplace there was a rocking chair and beside it another bench.

A doorway led to the other room and through it Austin could see three beds with lumpy mattresses held up by ropes, each with a bolster pillow and a bright quilt. Austin thought he recognized the squares as looking like material from Aunt Olivia's and Polly's dresses.

The whole cabin had the aroma of wood smoke and cornbread and pork, and Austin thought it smelled better than anything he could think of.

"It surely is little," Jefferson said as he sat himself down on the bench by the fireplace.

"Hush up, shrimp," Austin said.

Henry-James headed for the sideboard and picked up a tinder horn, a rock, and a piece of rag. "We likes it small. My grandpappy builded it that way on purpose way back when."

"Why?" Austin said.

"His daddy, he come right from Africa," Henry-James said. He began to beat the tinder horn against the rock and waited for a spark to fly out. He caught it with the rag and watched it form a flame. "His daddy tol' him to build these houses like the huts they live in back in Africa. Small and dark and warm."

"I'm not warm," Jefferson said. He pulled his chubby arms around himself. Although it had been a bright winter day, it was growing chillier as the sun began to set.

"That's why this child gonna make a fire," Henry-James said.

He took the flaming rag to the fireplace and lit the pyramid of wood that had already been laid. The room at once began to glow with a golden light that danced across Charlotte's face as she sat on the board floor nearby. Austin settled in on the rocker.

"That there is Daddy 'Lias's story chair," Henry-James said.

"Story?" Jefferson said. His face had an innocent shine as he scooted to the edge of the bench.

"Daddy Elias tells wonderful stories," Charlotte said.

"About what?" Jefferson and Austin both said at once.

"Jesus, mostly," she said. "That's why I hardly ever listen in church. Daddy Elias is so much better at it than Reverend Pullens."

"Then I'm staying until he tells us a story," Jefferson said. He crossed his little arms over his checkered shirt and gave his head a firm nod. Austin groaned inside.

"We can't stay that long," Charlotte said. "It's almost supper time and everyone will be wondering where we are."

"I don't care," Jefferson said. "We can eat supper here."

Charlotte shook her head at him. "Someone is sure to find us here, and then we'll never get to come back—ever!"

Jefferson was at once up and running to the door. Austin had to dive after him and wrestle him to the floor to keep him from bolting out and making for the Big House.

"Do you want to get us all caught?" Austin said to him.

"What are we going to do?" Charlotte said. "Even if we can get back to the house without anyone seeing us, they'll want to know where we've been."

She looked doubtfully at Jefferson as he wriggled out from under Austin and returned to his bench.

"And then you-know-who will t-e-l-l," Austin said.

"I get you back to the house safe," Henry-James said.

"And then?" Charlotte said.

Austin gnawed at a fingernail. It was a dilemma, all right. *There are sure to be questions. We'll have to think of something to tell Polly and Aunt Olivia and Mother.*

"What do *you* think, Austin?"

Austin looked up to find Charlotte and Henry-James watching him, as if they were waiting for him to speak.

"Don't you have any ideas?" Charlotte said. "This is all of our secret now."

All of ours. The words were warm in Austin's head.

"All right," he said. "We tell them we found Jefferson, you and I, Charlotte—that's true, right?"

"He found me, too," Jefferson said, pointing to Henry-James.

Austin frowned. "That's the hard part."

Charlotte looked at Jefferson. "We can't tell about Henry-James," she said.

Jefferson's eyes took on their devilish twinkle. "What will you give me if I don't tell?"

"Brat!" Austin said. "How about a punch if you *do?*"

Jefferson, of course, began to wail.

"We're going to have to let him come play with us," Charlotte said.

Jefferson stopped screaming and blinked at Charlotte. "I can play with you and Austin and him—every day?"

Austin scowled, but Henry-James and Charlotte both nodded.

Jefferson considered that. *"And* you have to promise to bring me *here* every day, too. I want to hear a story every day."

"Well, if that's what that chil' wants, that's what he gonna have," said a voice from the doorway. "A story every day."

✝ ⊹✠⊹ ✝

Chapter Thirteen

"**Y**ou're Daddy Elias," Jefferson said.

Henry-James's grandfather shuffled into the room, nodding his snowy head. Austin leaped from the rocker and swept his arm toward it.

"Here's your chair, sir," he said.

"You got it warmed up for me?" Daddy Elias said. He smiled his spoon-shaped smile at Austin until his eyes disappeared inside his soft, crinkly eyelids.

"You set down now, Daddy 'Lias," Henry-James said, scrambling up. "I'm gonna fetch you some boneset tea. Mama say give you that when you come in. Help you with that cough."

"Your mama fuss over me too much," Daddy Elias said. He sank down into the rocker.

With a heavy sigh, Bogie got up from under the table and went over to the chair, dropping himself onto the floor next to Daddy Elias like a sack of bones. Jefferson bounced across the room and climbed into the old man's lap.

"Jefferson, no!" Austin cried. The poor old man was so thin and brittle-looking that Austin was sure chunky Jefferson would break him.

But old Elias held up one hand to Austin while he wrapped the other one around Jefferson's tummy. "So you be wantin' you a story, young'un?" he said.

Jefferson nodded. "A long one, please—about Jesus."

The spoon-mouth formed an O. "About Jesus, now. Well, that's good, 'cause I don't know no other stories."

"Why?" Jefferson said.

"'Cause I don't need no other stories."

"Oh. Tell it, then."

Austin looked at the window once more. Long shadows were falling across the curtains, and Austin's stomach was fluttering nervously. Charlotte had scooted closer to Daddy Elias until she was at his feet. She looked up at him, the fire lighting up her face, and Polly and her father and the Big House seemed to be the furthest things from her mind. With a sigh, Austin sank down onto the bench.

"Once 'pon a time," Daddy Elias said, "they was a boy name of Jesus. He was 'long 'bout 12 years old when His mama and His daddy took Him on a long trip."

"Where did they go, Daddy?" Henry-James said from the table where he was stirring tea in a chipped blue cup.

Don't you know? Austin thought. *Haven't you heard this story before?* Austin himself hadn't, though, so he listened.

"They took theyselves to Jerusalem for the big feast. Mmmm-mmmm, and it was a feast to behold, too. They had them some plum puddin's and some Hoppin' John and some succotash—"

"And molasses candy?" Jefferson said.

"I reckon they did have molasses candy, yessir," Daddy Elias answered. "So Jesus and His mama and His daddy, they stayed there a time and they took theyselves to church and they pray real hard. And Jesus, He go to Sunday school with all them smart teachers—"

"Not like Polly," Jefferson said.

Daddy Elias didn't touch that one. "And when it come time for them to go on home, His mama and His daddy, they start off walkin', they's talkin' to the other folks as they go— and they's singin' and laughin' and jokin'—"

"And were they dancing, Daddy Elias?" Charlotte put in.

"I believe so, yes, ma'am. They was havin' theyselves such a good time, they plumb forgot 'bout Jesus. Well, course when she discover He ain't with them, His mama, she near to had a hissy fit."

"I know about those," Jefferson said.

"She say to her husband—he name's Joseph—she say, 'Joseph, we got to get our hind parts back there and find that boy!' So Mary and Joseph, they go runnin' back to they kin-folk and they be sayin', 'You seen Jesus? You seen our boy?' And hadn't nobody seen Him—not since they left Jerusalem."

"Almighty!" Henry-James exclaimed. He set the tea on the hearth and sat down beside Charlotte.

"Mmmm-hmmm," Daddy Elias said. "Now Mary, she like to tear herself up by this time, 'cause a whole day gone by now. So Joseph, he say, 'They ain't nothin' to do but we got to go back to Jerusalem and fetch that boy.' So they turns back to Jerusalem with they hearts right up here in they mouths, they so scared."

He stopped to take a sip of his tea, and Jefferson wiggled

impatiently on his lap. Austin found himself feeling a little anxious, too. He couldn't imagine being left behind on a trip by his parents—and he'd imagined just about everything.

"Well, they done search, and they look, and they dig. And don't you know, it take three days—*three days*—to find that boy. And you know where He was?"

"Playin' hide the switch with them other chilrun?" Henry-James said.

Daddy Elias shook his head and looked at Charlotte.

"Eating molasses candy under a tree?" she said.

"No, ma'am." Daddy Elias gave Jefferson a squeeze.

"He was cryin' on the street corner," Jefferson said with confidence. "He thought they were never coming back!"

"Oh, no, no. Lordy, no," Daddy Elias said.

"What happened?" Austin said. "Where was He?"

Daddy Elias observed Austin for a moment. His mouth went into its soft spoon smile, and his old faded eyes twinkled a little. "I bet you could figure it out, now."

Austin was startled, but he thought back over the story. "Was He still at Sunday school?"

"He was, for sure enough!" Daddy Elias cried. "He was sittin' right there in that church, right there on the floor with all them smart teachers all around Him. And do you know what?"

Four heads shook.

"They wasn't teachin' Him—no sirree. That boy Jesus—He teachin' *them!*"

Jefferson tugged at Daddy Elias's shirtfront. "How could He do that?" he said.

"I be comin' to that," Daddy Elias said. "Now, them teachers, they got they eyes poppin' out they heads, 'cause that boy Jesus He so smart. But His mama, she don't think

He so smart, uh-uh. She come flyin' in that church door and she go right up to Him and she say, 'Boy, what you think you doin'? Your daddy and me, we like to lose our mind lookin' for you, and here you be, just runnin' your mouth like there ain't no tomorrow. Why you do this?'"

Daddy Elias's voice had gone up into a shrill, mothering tone, and he was pointing his finger at all of them. "And that boy Jesus, He look up at His mama, and what you think He done?"

"I don't know," Jefferson said flatly. "He isn't like any other boy I ever heard of."

Daddy Elias chuckled from deep in his throat. "You right. He wasn't no regular boy. He didn't make up no lie for His mama like some other chilrun woulda done. No, sir, He look at His mama and He say, 'Mama, why you have to search for me? You don't know where I'm gonna be?' She say, 'How I'm gonna know that?' And He say, 'Mama, don't you know I'm gonna be right here in my daddy's house?' Now Mary, she don't know what that boy talkin' 'bout. This here was a church—this wasn't no house of no Joseph."

"Did she smack Him?" Jefferson said.

"No, sir," Daddy Elias said. "Mary, she just have this feelin' right here in her heart, and she know that even though she don't understand nothin' that this boy be sayin' to her, she know He just—different. And so she take Him back home to old Nazareth, and she just raise Him up best she can."

It was quiet then in the cabin, except for the snapping of the fire and the occasional thump of Bogie's tail on the floor. Charlotte and Henry-James and even Jefferson all looked into the fireplace as if they were letting the story settle over them like a warm quilt.

But Austin didn't feel settled at all. *We're going to go to the Big House and we're going to tell a big whopper of a lie. We're not going to do like that boy Jesus did.*

He closed his eyes and tried to imagine himself going into Uncle Drayton's library and telling him the truth. And then he tried to imagine Uncle Drayton understanding, the way Mary did.

Austin's eyes sprang open. *What if it doesn't work that way? What if Uncle Drayton makes it so we can never play together again—or come here and sit in this cabin and—*

No. This was different from the story about Jesus. They were going to have to tell half the truth and hope no one asked questions. That was all there was to it.

"Don't you think we'd better go?" he said.

Charlotte nodded reluctantly and got up from the floor.

Jefferson climbed down from Daddy Elias's lap and looked up at him. "We'll be back tomorrow," he said. "Because they promised that if I—"

"Let's go, shrimp," Austin said quickly. He grabbed Jefferson's hand and dragged him toward the door.

It was dark and quiet as Henry-James led them through the barnyard and left them on the back steps of the house. But inside, every lamp was lit and it was anything but quiet. They could hear Aunt Olivia and Polly competing to see who could be hysterical the loudest.

"Now you remember," Austin hissed to Jefferson, "you don't say a word—ever—about Henry-James or there will be no more stories and no more playing with us."

Jefferson obediently took Austin's hand and clamped his mouth shut.

"Where have you *been!*" Polly screeched when they

stepped inside the door.

Aunt Olivia took Charlotte roughly by the shoulder.

"Your father's gone off on business again, and here I am alone, responsible for you girls."

"It's my fault, Aunt Olivia," Austin said. "We heard Tot and Polly screa—calling for Jefferson, so we knew he must be lost. As you can see, we found him."

He gave Jefferson's hand a squeeze for good measure. Jefferson jerked his hand away, and for a horrible moment it looked as if he were going to unmask the whole plan. But he only stomped his foot and cried, "I'm going up to find my mother!" and disappeared up the stairs. Austin looked after him in amazement. What a wonderful idea.

"I'd better go with him," he said. "My mother must be worried sick."

Austin was at his mother's door before Aunt Olivia could even start yelling again.

Uncle Drayton isn't even here, Austin thought. *Maybe this will all work after all.*

But he skidded to a stop when he got into the room. Jefferson was already up on the bed beside his mother, chattering like a chickadee—and Kady was sitting in a chair at her side.

"Jefferson says you've had quite an afternoon," Mother said.

Austin looked hard at his little brother. Jefferson looked back, eyes round and blinking. Austin's insides began to cave in.

"We did," he said carefully.

"Seems he led Polly and Tot on a merry chase," Kady said.

Her mouth twitched.

"I had them all over the plantation," Jefferson said proudly.

"But why, Jefferson?" Mother said. "You were naughty to run like that."

Austin caught his breath. Jefferson blinked once again. "Because Polly has brown teeth," he said simply.

Kady coughed.

"That is no reason for you to frighten everyone to death!" Mother said. "Thank heaven Charlotte and Austin found you before you floated down the river in that boat!"

It was Austin's turn to cough. *Jefferson can lie like it's the absolute truth!* he thought.

"Well," Mother said, "you aren't going to do that again, are you?"

Jefferson shook his rumpled black head. "No, because I don't have to play with Polly in the afternoon anymore. I'm going to play with Austin."

Mother turned surprised brown eyes on Austin. "Really? Has Austin agreed to that?"

"Of course!" Austin said. "Charlotte and I will look after him."

"We're going to hear stories every day!"

"Jefferson!" Austin said—too loudly, he knew. "Tot's going to have your tea ready in the nursery. Go on now."

"And change your clothes first," Mother said, sniffing. "You smell like—is that pork?"

Austin held his breath as Jefferson scrambled down from the bed and crossed to the door. He stopped briefly before he left and gave Austin a smug smile. Austin didn't know whether to hug him or cuff him.

"Thank you for sitting with me, Kady," Mother was saying. "It was a nervous afternoon, but you were such a help."

"Think nothing of it, Aunt Sally," Kady said. "It was my pleasure. I'll read those books you gave me."

"Yes, do," Mother said faintly.

Austin could tell she was already drifting off to sleep, and he was glad. The fewer questions he had to answer, the better—especially until he had a chance to talk to Jefferson. There was no telling what story he had spun for her.

He left her room to go to his own. Out in the hall, Kady was waiting for him, smiling.

Why is she being nice to me all of a sudden? Austin thought. *Ever since this morning, I'm not poison anymore.*

"Stories, eh?" she said.

Austin's heart jumped. "Stories? Oh—Jefferson—yes— we're going to tell him stories—"

His words faded as she cocked one of her brown eyebrows. This time her mouth did break into a smile.

"I see," she said. "Well, don't worry about me. I won't tell anyone." She smiled again and swished off down the hall. At her door she looked back at Austin. "You're getting very good at keeping secrets, Austin."

She disappeared into her room. Austin stood there with his heart pounding. And then he shrugged. He *was* getting good at it. That must be what friends did for each other.

✠ ⋅✠⋅ ✠

ncle Drayton and Seton stayed gone for the rest of the week. Aunt Olivia whined at the dinner table every day that all this silly arguing with the North over the South's "peculiar institution" was what was keeping him away. Then she glared at Austin as if it were all his fault.

But that didn't bother Austin—because the rest of his life was getting better every day.

When Austin told Polly that he and Charlotte would look after Jefferson in the afternoons, she said it was about time someone gave her the help she deserved. But she didn't deliver quite so many mean looks after that.

Besides, Tot dumped a bowl of gumbo into Aunt Olivia's lap one day, and Aunt Olivia screamed that she was not fit to be a house servant, and Polly declared that she would lock herself in her room for the rest of her life if Mama took Tot away from her. So she had plenty of other things besides Austin and Jefferson to whine about.

Even better, Austin was able to use each morning in the

library to plan the next episode of their Charles Towne game. But making sure that no one caught Charlotte and Henry-James playing together was not a game, and Austin took that responsibility seriously.

At every cracking of a stick, Austin gave the whippoorwill call, and everyone ran for cover—only to emerge when it was discovered that it had been a passing deer. Henry-James told them that when the slaves had a meeting, they always dragged branches behind the last person to cover all their footprints. Austin made sure they did that every day. And each time, they met at a different place, which they agreed on before they parted in the late afternoons. They were spots far away from the eyes and ears of the rest of the plantation— upstairs in the spring house, beyond the garden, behind the family tomb. Although Henry-James was nervous about meeting near the tomb, he played courageously. Austin suggested that they meet the next day at the swamp.

"No, sir," Henry-James said promptly. "Bogie and me ain't playin' at no swamp."

"But you aren't afraid of anything," Austin said. "You even played here today—with all these dead people around."

"I ain't scared!" Henry-James said. "We can meet at your ol' swamp. But if you gets bitten by somethin' and you 'bout to die, don't come runnin' to me."

It really was the ideal time to meet at the swamp, because in their game, they'd already settled Charles Towne and begun to grow rice. There had been a snag when Austin explained how that was about the time when slaves were brought to South Carolina—so many that they outnumbered the white people.

"You be the slave," Jefferson had said, pointing to Henry-James.

"Why I got to be it?"

"Because," Jefferson said, "you already know how."

Henry-James flung down the branch he'd been using for a cane. "I don't wanna play this game no more," he said.

Bogie growled under his breath.

Austin watched Charlotte nervously. She looked as if she were ready to give it all up, too, if Henry-James walked away.

"Who wants to pretend something they already are?" Austin said quickly. "I think *we* ought to all be the slaves and let Henry-James be the master. After all, there are always more slaves anyway."

"You won't beat us, will you?" Jefferson said.

"What are you talking about?" Austin said. "Uncle Drayton doesn't beat his slaves!"

"Yes, he does. Polly is always saying if Tot doesn't straighten up, her daddy's going to take her out and whip her."

"I don't want to be no slave owner anyhow," Henry-James said.

Austin gave his brain a frantic search. "All right, then," he said, "let's skip to the Indians."

Faces brightened and were immediately painted with mud for war paint, and the game went on with the settlers, Henry-James and Jefferson, seizing the Indians' land and Charlotte and Austin the Yamasees taking them on in the Yamasee War.

Although the settlers won, the dead Indians were allowed to come back the next day as Blackbeard's pirates robbing ships along the Carolina coast. Everyone had a turn at walking the plank, and then Blackbeard was killed. Then, of course, they re-enacted the Revolutionary War, which took part of an afternoon, and the discovery of the cotton gin, which lasted until almost evening. But that only led to more slavery, and they were stuck again.

That was the day they met at the swamp, and Austin had a brilliant idea. "None of us has to be a slave *or* a slave owner," he told his players. "Two of us can be Patty Rollers, and two of us can be the ghosts of slaves they turned in."

They loved it. Charlotte donated her petticoats for ghost costumes, and she and Austin donned them and hid among the cypress trees. When Henry-James and Jefferson, the deliciously evil Patty Rollers, came on the scene calling for their lost slaves, Charlotte and Austin began a chorus of "Wooooo!" The best part of all was when Bogie threw back his flabby-skinned head and howled for all he was worth. It sent chills up even Austin's backbone.

The Patty Rollers had been spooked for about the fifth time that day, and it was time to switch roles.

"Just put this petticoat over your head," Charlotte instructed Jefferson. "You can see right through it, the material is so thin."

Austin handed his costume to Henry-James and grinned as he struggled to get into it.

"Don't you be laughin' at me," Henry-James said with a scowl. "Turn your head, or I'll have Bogie on you."

Austin didn't stop grinning, but he did swivel his head the other way. He caught a glimpse of something white in the cypress trees where he and Charlotte had just been.

"Did we leave one of your petticoats back there?" he said.

Charlotte shook her silky head. "No. I only had two. Polly is the one who wears five."

Austin squinted. "Then what was that I saw?"

Henry-James poked his head through his ghost garb and stared. Austin saw his eyes widen for a fraction of a second.

"I don't see nothin," he said.

"I don't either, now," Austin said, "but I did a minute ago. Didn't you, Charlotte?"

"All right, Jefferson," she said. "Practice your 'Wooooo!'"

Austin looked across the swamp again, but the trees were still and bare.

"You gettin' too wrapped up in this game," Henry-James said, poking him.

"I guess so," Austin said.

But none of the games, no matter how exciting, ever matched storytelling time. Each day as the children neared the end of the afternoon's adventure, the enthusiasm began to turn into anticipation of the next tale about Jesus. As soon as Slave Street came in sight, they all bolted for it.

They were always waiting with the old man's tea hot when he walked in the door, though Jefferson could barely allow him to sit down before he was in his lap. Austin joined Charlotte, Henry-James, and Bogie on the floor after the first day, and he learned that they asked questions not because they didn't know the answers, but because that was just part of the fun of the storytelling.

He told them all about Jesus eating with the tax collectors and the sinners and telling those ol' Pharisees to "mind they own business 'cause He got work to do healin' these poor miserable people." There were the ones about a good Samaritan helping a man everyone hated, about Jesus scolding the people for being mean to a sinner woman "when they wasn't no better theyselves," and about Him healing people with leprosy that no one else would even get near.

Austin was always restless when it was time for the "white chilrun" to return to the Big House.

I like this man Jesus, he always wanted to say. *I want to hear more.* Of course, there could be no saying that in front of Jefferson. But one evening as Henry-James ushered Charlotte and Jefferson to the fence, Austin lingered behind.

"You got a puzzle all in pieces in your mind," Daddy Elias said to him.

It *did* feel that way. "How did you get to be so smart?" Austin asked.

The old white head shook, and the spoon-smile was soft on his lips. "Oh, I ain't smart, Massa Austin. You the one that's smart. Old Daddy 'Lias, he just listen to the Lord, that's all—just like a friend."

"Does He talk to you?" Austin said.

"Through them stories He does," Daddy Elias said. "You just think about them stories, 'cause Jesus, He talkin' right to you every time."

Austin could almost feel the puzzle pieces rattling around in his head. "But how? I don't understand."

"They's waitin' for you out there."

Austin turned to see Ria outlined in the doorway.

It was the only time Austin had seen her since the first day he'd visited Slave Street. She gave him a long look now with her serious black eyes, and then she hurried over to the fireplace and poked at the fire.

Austin moved quickly toward the doorway. It felt as if he'd been in her house without permission.

He thought a lot that night about what Daddy Elias had said, so much that he couldn't get to sleep.

I can't get enough of the stories, he thought. *Everyone is always asking questions and laughing and hollering out answers. If I could just hear them by myself—without having to be in the cabin or in church—*

Church.

Of course! Reverend Pullens read the stories to them on Sundays, right out of the Bible.

The clock was just striking 11:00. Austin tossed back the quilt, pulled on a pair of trousers over his underdrawers, and crept out into the chilly hall. Just as he'd known it would be, the house was dark and quiet, but he didn't mind the damp cold as he padded, barefoot, down the stairs and across the hall to the library.

But he stopped before he got there. A faint flicker of light escaped from the crack, and from within voices murmured—Aunt Olivia's and Polly's.

"I have enough to worry about, what with Sally and those boys," Aunt Olivia said snappishly, "and your father gone—"

Austin turned to go back up the steps. He'd heard all this before.

"—and Charlotte practically hopeless. I'm almost worn to a frazzle."

Austin stopped. *Charlotte—hopeless?* The words stabbed at him as if Aunt Olivia had thrown them in a game of mumblety-peg.

"I can't be concerned with one slave girl."

"It isn't just 'one slave girl'!" Polly said. "It's Tot!"

Her tone rooted Austin to his spot. Was narrow-eyed, bossy, selfish Polly about to cry?

"Don't be silly," Aunt Olivia snapped. "She's nothing but a clumsy thing—and a stupid one at that."

"How would you feel if someone took Mousie away from you?"

"Mousie doesn't pour food into my lap and try to start fires in the bedroom."

"Tot doesn't mean to!"

"Will that matter when this house goes up in flames?"

Austin heard a loud choking sound.

"Oh, now, girl, don't cry," Aunt Olivia said.

"Tot's been with me since I was five years old!" Polly wailed in a broken, sniffing voice. "She's my only friend in this world. Kady and Charlotte both hate me!"

"They don't hate you, child! They're both just jealous of you, is all," Aunt Olivia scolded her.

Jealous? Austin thought. *Of what?*

"Why would they be jealous of me, Mama?" Polly said. "Kady has prettier hair, and Charlotte has nicer teeth."

"But you know how important it is to care about your looks and your manners. It makes no difference how beautiful Kady is. If she doesn't care about getting herself a nice husband, it isn't going to happen. And Charlotte is so backward and shy, we'll be lucky to convince her to talk to *us*, much less a boy. But you're working so hard, my precious. And that's why I want you to have the best servant possible. Do you think that awkward Tot is going to be of any help to you whatsoever when you start receiving gentlemen?"

"I don't care!" Polly cried. "I won't have anyone to talk to! You have Daddy, and Charlotte plays with Austin now, and Kady is always in Aunt Sally's room—"

"What?"

Aunt Olivia's reply cracked out like a whip, and it jolted even Austin. He stiffened.

"Every afternoon Kady sits with Aunt Sally and they read books and talk. It sounds dreadfully boring to me, but at least it's something. If I didn't have Tot—"

"When did this start?"

"Ever since Charlotte and Austin started looking after Jefferson. But Mama—"

"We'll have to see about *that!*" Aunt Olivia said.

"What about Tot, though?"

"Oh, Polly, for heaven's sake! If you will cease to bother me about this, Tot can stay with you for now. But the next time she does something to endanger the welfare of this household, she is gone."

"Gone—where?" Polly said tearfully. "You don't mean sell her?"

"I certainly do."

"Mama, no. You can't sell her!"

"It's up to your daddy anyway," Aunt Olivia said impatiently. "You just tell that girl to watch her step, and then you won't have to worry about it."

There was a rustle of petticoats, and Austin uprooted himself from the floor and dashed lightly back up the steps. He had almost reached his room when a door down the hall creaked open. His mother's room was closer than his, and he dove into it and shut the door behind him.

"Austin?" Mother said sleepily. "Is that you?"

"Yes," he said, fighting for breath.

"What are you doing, son?" she said. "Is something wrong?"

"No," he said.

What do I tell her? he thought frantically.

"Austin?" she said.

"I'm all right, Mother. I was just—looking for a Bible."

She laughed her lilting laugh, which quickly turned into a cough. Austin got her some water from the pitcher and sat on the edge of the bed. The comfort he always got from being with her didn't wrap itself around him this time.

"You need some boneset tea for that cough," Austin said.

She lay back on her pillows and smiled through the thin moonlight. "You are a breed apart, Austin Hutchinson," Mother said. "First you come in here in the middle of the night looking for a Bible. Then you start prescribing medicines I've never even heard of. Where did you—?"

"Do you have a Bible?" Austin cut in.

"I do."

"Do you ever read about Jesus?" Austin said.

"Sometimes. Why?"

"I want to read His stories," Austin said. "We've heard them in church—" He paused, knowing he had better be careful. He'd already almost slipped up by mentioning the tea.

"Ah, and you want to do some study on your own?" Mother said. "You are so much like your father."

"May I borrow your Bible?" he said.

"Why don't we read the stories together? Perhaps you could come in after supper."

"Do I have to bring Jefferson?" Austin said. Reading the Bible stories was sure to bring comments about the way Daddy Elias told them.

"I don't think we could get Jefferson to sit still long enough!"

Austin nodded guiltily and made for the door. And he hoped the moonlight wasn't bright enough to reveal his secrets, which were smeared all over his face.

✝ ✙ ✝

Chapter Fifteen

*A*s Austin sat looking out the library window the next day, he couldn't concentrate on a plan for the afternoon's play.

Those puzzle pieces Daddy Elias was talking about, he thought to himself. *They're all the questions I can't ask Mother—or anybody—anymore.*

For almost the first time since his father had left, Austin thought about him. *Would he be able to answer all these questions—like could it be that Polly really cares about somebody besides herself?*

And had Aunt Olivia really meant she would sell Tot? Would Uncle Drayton sell a person because she was clumsy and made mistakes?

Austin looked around at the library with its rich, shiny volumes and its elegant mahogany desk and its masculine, leathery smell of Uncle Drayton. He was strong, charming, friendly, and handsome—the leader everyone looked up to. He was the kind of man Austin wanted to be.

Austin shook his head at his reflection in the window. No, it was Aunt Olivia who was the evil one. She was probably telling Polly all that stuff just to scare her.

When Uncle Drayton comes back, Austin thought, *we'll just see about that!*

He expected to feel better, but the thought of Uncle Drayton coming home produced a few more puzzle pieces he couldn't fit together. *Will he find out Charlotte has been playing with Henry-James? Will he discover that I've been helping them? Will that mean our friendships will be over?*

That was a thought too terrible to think about. But even that was chased out of his mind that afternoon during dinner. They were just about to start dessert when the front door knocker clattered.

At first Aunt Olivia only frowned and ignored it, but when the racket went on, she stabbed her spoon impatiently into her bowl and said, "Will no one get that? Where is Mousie?"

"You sent her upstairs to get your shawl," Kady said.

Aunt Olivia looked fitfully around the dining room. "Go, Tot," she said. "Try not to break anything on the way."

Austin held his breath as Tot made her way out the door, but all the china stayed mercifully on its shelves.

When the door was flung open again, Tot stood in the doorway puffing like a train engine.

"Well, what is it?" Aunt Olivia said.

Tot jerked her head toward the doorway and it darkened with two figures. Austin put his napkin up to his mouth.

It was Barnabas Brown and Irvin Ullmann. Austin ducked his head as Aunt Olivia stood up and bustled toward them.

"What is it?" she said. "Is there trouble with one of our darkies? Mr. Ravenal isn't here, you know."

"We know that, ma'am," Barnabas said, tugging at his thin beard. "That's why we come—to warn you."

Aunt Olivia clutched at her throat. "Warn us about what?"

"Mr. Ravenal's body slave—"

"Seton?" Kady said. She pushed back from the table.

"He done run off from Mr. Ravenal while he was way over at St. Stephen's Parish. He's gone to look for him, and that's why he sent us."

Austin felt as if his stomach had been stabbed.

"Seton?" Aunt Olivia said. "That's ridiculous! He's as loyal to Drayton as I am!"

"Mr. Ravenal, he's afraid there might be trouble with your other slaves if that darky tries to come back to see his family once more."

"Seton doesn't have any family here," Kady said.

Austin looked at her quickly. Her voice was stiff, and her fingers were curled so tightly on the back of her chair that her knuckles looked like a row of pearls.

"But he's got a brother at the Singletons'!" Polly said. "Tot just whispered it to me."

Kady gave Tot a glare so fierce that Austin suddenly had a vision of *her* selling the poor black girl.

"Did Mr. Ravenal send instructions?" Aunt Olivia said.

"You're supposed to let us patrol your plantation until he gets back," Barnabas said. "Irvin here and I will catch that thief if he tries to come back here."

"Why is he a thief?" Austin said. "Did he steal something?"

The minute he said it, he wanted to dive under the table. For the first time, the two Patty Rollers looked at him, straight on, and a glimmer crossed Barnabas Brown's face.

I hope they don't recognize me! Austin thought as he

turned his head away again. *Or there's going to be trouble—with or without Seton!*

"They called him a thief," Kady said, "because he 'stole himself.' He 'belongs' to my father, so running away is like stealing."

"It *is* stealing!" Irvin growled. "And by golly, we'll catch the little cuffee at it!"

"Charlotte," Aunt Olivia said, "you are not to play outdoors today, do you hear? It's too dangerous."

Charlotte didn't answer. Aunt Olivia apparently didn't expect her to because she turned again to the Patty Rollers.

"I appreciate your help," she said. "I hope you catch him. He deserves punishment—after all Mr. Ravenal has done for him."

She ushered them both out the door then, and Kady followed and disappeared up the front stairs.

"Tot, let's go to my room!" Polly said shrilly. "I don't feel safe anywhere else."

They clung to each other and somehow managed to get out of the dining room.

"What happens when one of your father's slaves runs away?" Austin asked Charlotte.

She shrugged. "I don't know. None of them has ever left before."

"That's because your father treats them so well."

Charlotte looked down at her patent leather shoes.

"Are you scared, too, like Polly is?" Austin said.

"Polly isn't scared. She just likes to play-act. Now, Kady— I think she's scared."

"Why?"

"Because she's afraid something bad is going to happen

to Seton, and maybe his brother, still hiding out in the swamp—"

Her mouth suddenly stopped moving, as if she'd said more than she should have.

"What's the matter?" Austin said.

"Nothing," she said. She looked up at the ceiling.

Austin felt a light flickering in his brain. "Charlotte, is Brawley—that one slave who ran away from the Singletons'— is he Seton's brother? Was that him we saw that day in the swamp—both those days?"

Charlotte twisted her foot on the floor. "We should be talking about how we're going to get word to Henry-James that we can't play today."

"I'll go tell him," Austin said impatiently, "but I want to know—"

"You can't go. Mama said we're to stay inside."

"She said *you* are," Austin said. "I don't think she cares much what happens to me." He drew closer to her. "But you said Brawley—is Seton's *brother*? Did you know that was him hiding in the swamp? Did you know they were both going to escape?"

"You really do ask too many questions sometimes, Austin," she said. She pulled up a layer of ruffles on her dress and began to twist them around her finger. Austin watched her in dismay.

"You only do that with your finger when there's something wrong," Austin said. "Why can't you tell me?"

"Because I'm not supposed to!" Charlotte cried. "Kady says it's just between us. It's a secret!"

"But why is Kady—? Doesn't she believe in slavery?"

"I can't tell you! Kady said not to. She doesn't know if we can trust you yet!"

Austin felt his chest pinch—hard. "Do *you* trust me?"

"You have to go find Henry-James now," she said. But she wouldn't look at him. Her eyes, so much like his, were aimed straight down at the floor. "And you should tell him about the Patty Rollers, too, and Seton."

"I'm surprised you trust me to do that," Austin said. His throat felt as thick as a piece of wood, and so did his heart— one that was about to split in two.

He turned with a jerk to go. Mousie stood in the doorway, clutching a pink shawl, and she jumped when Austin saw her.

"Where's missus?" she said in her tiny voice.

"I don't know," Austin said. "No one tells me anything."

He brushed past her and headed for the stairs, too stunned to do anything else.

Austin leaned against the wall at the top of the steps and caught his breath. She didn't trust him. He'd thought he finally had a friend, but she was just like the rest of them.

She only played with me so she could be with Henry-James, he thought woodenly. *They don't care about me at all.*

He pulled himself away from the door and straightened his narrow shoulders. *Then I don't care about them either,* he told himself.

But even as he stiffened his inner resolve and headed for his room, he knew it wasn't true—he *did* care about them. The pinching in his chest told him that, along with the happiness he'd felt these last days.

Henry-James is my friend, he thought.

As he stood with his hand on the doorknob, Austin felt the pieces come loose in his head again. They hurt, rattling around in there, but he knew one thing. He still had to go and warn Henry-James.

He pushed open his bedroom door, intent on getting his jacket, and his heart sank. Jefferson was sitting cross-legged on the bed.

"Where are we going today?" he said in a loud whisper.

"Nowhere," said a voice in the hall. "Your mama wants to see you."

It was Kady, standing in the hall. Austin's mind began to reel.

I have to get out—soon! And I can't take Jefferson. This is too much for him to know.

"Austin, I'm so sorry," Sally Hutchinson said when they got to her room.

Austin stared at her blankly.

"Kady was just telling me that you've spent some time with Seton. I know you must be heartbroken that he's run away."

That news traveled like a speeding train, Austin thought bitterly.

"I'm all right," he said. "But I do have some things to take care of outside."

"Not today," Mother said firmly. She coughed and then caught her breath. "After what Kady has told me, I think it's far too risky for you to be out and about. Why don't we do some of that Bible reading we were talking about last night?"

Austin couldn't help but glare at Kady. It certainly hadn't taken her long to convince his mother that he, too, should be "held prisoner" in the house. But Kady's eyes sprang open at her aunt and for a second, she looked confused.

"Oh, Aunt Sally," she said, "I think my mother is exaggerating the dangers. Even if Seton were to come back here, it would take him until tonight to travel from

St. Stephen's Parish on foot. It's silly to—"

"Mothers are silly creatures," Sally Hutchinson said. "Would you be kind enough to help Jefferson find something to do while I spend some time reading with Austin?"

Kady hesitated.

"If it's too much trouble—" Mother started to say.

But Kady shook her dark curls and took Jefferson by the hand. "It's fine, really. I'll find you my old kaleidoscope, Jefferson, and I think there's a Jacob's Ladder. That will be more fun than going . . . where were you going today?"

Austin gave Jefferson a sharp look, but he was gazing at Kady. "Behind the sugar cane mill," he said cheerfully. "Nobody can see us there."

"Those are the best places to play, aren't they?" Kady said, and she led him out of the room.

Not anymore, they aren't, Austin thought with his teeth clenched together. *You're never playing with us again, Jefferson. You can't keep your mouth shut.*

Austin had to dig his feet into the rug to keep from running after them and warning Jefferson once again. *He's probably mentioned Henry-James's name six times by now.*

"Austin, you look so upset," his mother said. "Come here. Let's talk."

With one more wistful glance toward the door, Austin went to the edge of the big four-poster bed and sat down.

"I'm so proud of you," she said.

"Why?"

"Because you've taken such good care of your brother since we've been here. I know he can be a trial."

Austin's chest pinched so hard that he could barely breathe. *Please, let's talk about something else,* he thought.

"And the way you're so worried about this slave—what's his name, Seton?"

Austin nodded.

"But you know, if he does get away successfully, he's going to have a much better life. That's what your father and I have been trying to tell people all these years."

Austin scanned the room with his eyes, looking for another subject, and his glance fell on the Bible on the table beside the bed.

"Weren't we going to read together?" he said.

She smiled and patted his hand. "Of course. You said you wanted to read about Jesus."

Austin picked up the Bible and sat uneasily beside her.

"What do you want to know?" she said.

"Did Jesus have any friends?" Austin said listlessly.

"Ah," Mother said. "I know just what we should read."

Austin crossed his arms and tried to listen.

"'And it came to pass'," she read, "'that he saw two ships standing by the lake, but the fishermen were gone out of them.'"

What is Henry-James going to do when we don't show up?

"'When he had left speaking, he said unto Simon, Launch out into the deep, and let down your nets.'"

How much has Jefferson told Kady?

"'Simon said unto him, Master, we have toiled all night and have taken nothing.'"

But Kady trusted Charlotte with her secrets. Why is she trying to get our secrets out of Jefferson?

"'And when they had this done, they enclosed a great multitude of fishes, and their net broke.'"

And what's going to happen to Seton if they find him? Surely Uncle Drayton won't do anything terrible to him. Or to Henry-James, if he finds out about us.

"'And when Simon Peter saw it, he fell down at Jesus' knees saying, "Depart from me, for I am a sinful man, O Lord."' Isn't that something, Austin?"

Austin drifted back to her.

"What?" he said.

"How Jesus chose such misfits for His friends."

"What's a misfit?" Austin said.

"Just what it sounds like. Somebody who doesn't quite fit."

Austin grunted. "Just like me," he muttered.

But she began to cough, and she turned the Bible over and sat up. It still sounded like gravel coming from her chest.

"I wish I could stop this," she said. She shook her head. "Perhaps I do need some of that—what was it you told me last night?"

I'm not going to make that mistake again! Austin thought. *I almost had to tell her where I heard about it.*

And then an idea sprang into his mind, right up out of the litter of puzzle pieces.

"Boneset tea," Austin said. He jumped from the bed. "I'm going to go get you some right now!"

"Austin, you don't have to—" she called to him.

But he was already out the door and halfway down the stairs.

✝ ✜ ✝

anaan Grove was strangely quiet as Austin raced from the Big House and across the barnyard toward the sugar cane mill.

He took a sharp turn at the blacksmith's shop and careened toward the sugar mill. But there was no one there.

Austin looked around wildly. "Henry-James?" he hissed.

No answer.

He gave a whippoorwill call. There was nothing in return.

Hauling air into his lungs, Austin broke for Slave Street. The grayness was gathering overhead for rain, and the cabin-lined dirt road looked lonely and grim as he ran down it. He rounded the turn and made it to Henry-James's cabin in a few leaps. He began to call his name before he got to the door.

"You can stop your yellin'," said a voice from inside, "'cause Henry-James ain't here."

Austin pulled the door open. "Daddy Elias? Why aren't you working?"

Daddy Elias was in his rocker, wrapped in a quilt made of

Ravenal dresses and cradling his chipped blue cup in his hand. "Ria tol' them I too sick to be workin' today," he said. He coughed and took a sip from his cup.

"You want me to poke the fire?" Austin said.

"Now that would be nice."

Austin gave the faltering flames a few jabs and threw on two pine knots, and the fire perked up. All the while, his mind was picking up puzzle pieces and then throwing them back down.

Should I ask him where Henry-James is? Should I just get some boneset tea and leave? Should I tell him *about Seton and the Patty Rollers?*

"Now that there is a downright guilty look on your face, Massa Austin."

Austin looked up from the fire, his cheeks hot. "Guilty?"

"When you done something you shouldn't ought to done—but you just didn't know which way to turn at the time."

"I *don't* know, Daddy Elias!" Austin said.

"Well now, I knows how that feels," said the old man. He shook his woolly-white head.

"You couldn't. You always know what to do."

"Onliest thing I knows is to go to Jesus."

"I don't know how to do that," Austin said. He went anxiously to the window and peered out. If only Henry-James would come home.

"Sure you do. Didn't you look at them stories like I tol' you?"

Austin looked at him. "Yes, I did."

"Mmmm-hmmm. And what did you find?"

"Nothing that will help me now!" Austin said. "I have to find Henry-James."

"I think you got to find Massa Austin first. Now why don't you just set yourself down right here by Daddy 'Lias?"

Austin could feel his throat getting tight. This wasn't helping. He had to go!

But Austin sat down miserably. Maybe he could just wait a few minutes more for Henry-James.

"Now then," the old man said, his mouth forming into its spoon shape, "what did you find in them stories?"

"Jesus helping some fishermen catch fish," Austin said.

"And what did ol' Simon Peter do when he saw his nets all plumb full up with shrimp and oysters and catfish?"

Austin thought half-heartedly. "He . . . fell down on his knees in front of Jesus . . . and told Him he was a sinful man."

"And then what happen?"

"I don't know. We didn't go that far." Austin started to get up. "My mother is coughing just like you, Daddy Elias. May I have some of your boneset tea?"

"What you *think* happen next?"

There was no point in saying he didn't know. Austin closed his eyes and tried to hurry an image into place.

"He said He *wanted* to be with the sinners, and could they be friends," he said.

The spoon smile opened up. "That's right," he said. "Now you just whisper, 'Jesus, we be friends—show me the way.' And He will, sure enough."

"Jesus isn't going to want to be my friend," Austin said. "Nobody really wants to. You know what, Daddy Elias? I just don't *fit* around here. I'm . . . I'm a misfit!"

He hadn't meant to say all of that, and he hadn't meant to almost cry either. He got to his feet and wiped at his eyes with the backs of his hands.

"I really have to go," he said.

"Then get you some of that there tea for your mama,"

Daddy Elias said quietly.

He pointed to a tin on the table, and Austin went toward it with his eyes still blurry. He was dipping the spoon into it when a chorus of voices broke out in the street.

"Ah, Lord! Lord have mercy!" they sang.

Another voice answered—a little unsure of itself but strong and clear.

"Oh, my brother done move!" it sang.

"Lord, have mercy!"

"My brother done move his campin' ground! Gonna meet my brother there tonight!"

Austin pulled open the curtain and felt his jaw fall.

"That's Henry-James singing!" he cried. He yanked open the door and sprang out onto the porch.

"Lord, have mercy!" the chorus sang, clapping their hands over their heads.

"Gonna meet my brother there!" Henry-James answered back.

"Henry-James!" Austin called out, but the group of singers just danced by. Even Bogie trotted along at Henry-James's side, as if he had urgent business to attend to.

"This is *important!*" Austin shouted.

As the chorus of checkered-capped women kept chanting "Lord, have mercy," Henry-James did shift his black eyes toward the porch, but he shook his head at Austin and kept going. What he had to do was obviously more important.

What? Austin thought hopelessly. *Sing some old song?*

And then he knew. It wasn't just some old song. There was going to be a secret meeting. Austin could tell him there.

Austin took off after the singing slaves. He'd barely gone two steps when he felt a hand on his shoulder.

"This ain't no place for you," someone said next to his ear.

Austin stared up at a stern face close to his.

"Ria!" Austin said. "I was just following Henry-James."

"You don't belong in no slave-singin'. You go on back to the Big House now, and you stay there."

"But I need to tell somebody. There might be trouble if—"

Ria's eyes went into slits, and Austin thought her cheek-bones would come through her skin, her face was so rigid. "Ain't gonna be no trouble unless you makes it," she said. "Now git on home!"

She let go of his shoulder, but she didn't move, and he knew she was going to watch him. By now Henry-James and the others had gone off in the opposite direction from the house, and Austin had no choice but to do as she said.

By the time he reached the back porch, the singing was nothing but a memory in his ears. He stood on tiptoes and craned to see where they'd gone, but the plantation was quiet and the damp chill was settling with the darkness over every-thing. A misty rain began to fall, and Austin could see almost nothing beyond the stable yard.

When he stepped inside the back door, shaking droplets out of his hair, a shadowy figure crept out from under the steps.

Charlotte motioned him over. "Hurry!" she whispered. "I have to talk to you!"

Cautiously, Austin joined her under the steps. She curved into a corner, and all Austin could see were her honey-brown eyes, shining like two pools of concern.

"Did you find him?" she said.

"Yes, but I couldn't talk to him. He was singing everybody

to a meeting. Ria wouldn't let me go with them. She said a slave-singin' was no place for me."

He didn't add what he was thinking—that maybe this whole plantation was no place for him.

"She doesn't know you," Charlotte whispered. "When she does, she'll trust you."

Then why don't you? Austin shouted inside his head. But he said, "Where do they usually hold their meetings?"

"Different places," Charlotte said. "Did you hear the words to the song?"

Austin scrambled back through his mind. "Something about 'My brother done change his . . . campin' ground.'"

"Camping ground." Charlotte's eyebrows puckered.

"Is there a place where they sleep outside—in a tent?"

"No, *shhh*. Listen," she said. "There's one song they sing about dying and they call it going to the camping ground."

Austin felt a chill. "Do they have a cemetery?"

Charlotte nodded. "But they would never meet there. It's right out in the open, over by the carriage house."

"Where else would they go after they're dead?"

"By then, they're just spirits," Charlotte said. "They don't need to meet anymore!"

Austin grabbed her arm. "Spirits? Ghosts! Where do the Patty Rollers think the slaves' ghosts come back? The one place they'd never go?"

Charlotte's eyes lit up the darkness. "The swamp! I told you, the slaves don't like to go there either."

"But Henry-James did, with us." Austin paused. "I guess you're right. He's only 12. They wouldn't pay any attention to him."

"But if they were following his singing, they're already

trusting him to take Seton's place."

"Then I have to go to the swamp!" Austin stood up, and Charlotte snatched in the dark for his hand.

"I thought Aunt Sally said you weren't supposed to go outside either!" she hissed.

"How did you know that?"

"Kady told me."

Austin groaned. "What else did she tell you? Did she say that Jefferson blabbed everything to her?"

"Jefferson? No. She handed him over to me right after she left your mother's room, and I haven't seen her since."

"Where is he now?" Austin said.

Charlotte's eyes danced. "He's asleep. I told Polly it was her turn when he wakes up—and then I hid. She's been looking for me all over the house. I have to move every five minutes."

"I'm going to the swamp," Austin said. "Somebody has to warn them!"

He ducked out from under the steps and crept quickly to the back door and slipped out. Charlotte followed.

"What are you doing?" he hissed to her.

"I'm coming with you!" she whispered back.

"You aren't supposed to go out!"

"Neither are you—what's the difference?"

"You don't have a wrap."

"I'll get a blanket in the stables. Come on!"

And grabbing Austin's hand, she pulled him off into the mist.

✜ ❖ ✜

Chapter Seventeen

*A*s Austin ran through the rainy night with Charlotte, both of them wrapped in horsy-smelling blankets, he wasn't sure which was moving faster—his mind or his legs.

We have to get to the slaves before the Patty Rollers do. I saw how they treated that slave at the train station! And we have to do it before supper so no one discovers Charlotte is gone.

He had to slow both his steps and his thoughts when he started to smell the swamp's dank odor. The ground would be getting more slippery and the branches hanging lower, and it was going to take their full attention so they wouldn't slide off into the mud—or worse. He kept his eyes down.

"I can't see whether there are any footprints or not," he whispered to Charlotte.

"There wouldn't be anyway," she said. "Remember, they always drag branches behind them to cover their tracks."

Austin stopped abruptly, and Charlotte, too, halted and turned to look at him in horror.

146

"We didn't do that!" she whispered.

"We were in such a hurry to get here, I forgot!"

"Start now. If anyone gets this far, they'll think we turned back."

"Right. Who would go into the swamp at night anyway?" Austin said. He laughed, but he knew it sounded nervous. With the shadows dripping off the Spanish moss and the shapes of the cypress rising up out of the mist like suspicious heads, it wasn't quite as inviting as it was in the daytime.

"Here," Charlotte whispered. She handed him a branch, and Austin trailed it behind him as they made their way in silence until Austin caught a glimmer through the trees.

"What's that light?" he whispered.

"It's their torches, Austin! They're here!"

She grabbed his arm, and together they hurried down the muddy path. As they made the last curve, Austin let an "oh!" slip from his throat.

Pine knot torches lined the edge of the swamp like candles, casting a flickering orange glow on the deep-brown faces below them. Bodies, huddled together and covered in faded ginghams and torn calicos, swayed as one. Woolly and scarf-clad heads bobbed and shiny lips hummed—and every eye was closed.

"*Shhh!*" Charlotte whispered.

"What are they doing?" Austin said. "Is that some kind of African—?"

"They're praying!"

Even as she said it, Austin heard a low molasses voice murmur, "Sweet Jesus."

"*I just goes to Jesus,*" Daddy Elias had said.

That's what they're doing, Austin thought. *They think He's right here.*

And for a moment, Austin was sure He was. It was as if some-one were here standing guard, so they could meet in peace.

With a jerk, Austin remembered why they were here.

"Do you see Henry-James?" he whispered.

Charlotte pointed, and Henry-James himself raised his head. His eyes bulged.

Beside him, Ria, too, looked up, and her face pinched in like an ax head. When she stood up, Austin wasn't sure this had been a good idea.

Most of the heads had come up by now, and a fearful murmur rippled through the slaves.

"I thought I tol' you to go home and stay there!" Ria said in a hoarse whisper.

"The Patty Rollers," Austin stammered, "they're patrolling Canaan Grove all day and night until my uncle comes back. Seton has run away."

They all stared as if their faces were made of stone.

"We already know that," Henry-James said.

Now the muttering raced through the group, and it was angry. Austin felt himself shrinking under the horse blanket. His face, he knew, was flaming like one of their torches.

"Come on," Charlotte whispered to him. She tugged at his blanket, and Austin started to follow her. But he stopped and looked back.

"I'm sorry," he said. "I was only trying to help."

"We don't need no help!" Henry-James said. "Go on 'fore you leads them Patty Rollers right to us." He glanced quickly at his mother, who had sat back down among the group. Austin's eyes followed, and he choked back a gasp. Right behind her, where Austin hadn't been able to see him before, was Brawley.

Charlotte gave another tug, and this time Austin followed her.

"They had Brawley with them!" Austin said as they hurried back down the path. "He must have been hiding with them all this time! But how did they find out about Seton and the Patty Rollers?"

Charlotte just shook her head.

"Tot—do you think? I know she isn't very smart, but she could have—"

Charlotte sniffed, and Austin looked at her. Her face was damp with the mist. But two rivulets that he knew were tears worked their way down her cheeks.

"Are you crying?" he said.

She nodded miserably.

"Why?"

"Do you always have to ask so many questions, Austin?" she said. A loud hiccup burst from her, and she turned her streaked, puckered face to him. "I've never had Henry-James angry with me before! I'm afraid he's never going to speak to me again!"

"But you were only trying to help."

"Leave me alone!" she cried.

She pulled her blanket across her chest with one hand and snatched up her skirt with the other and took off running down the path away from the swamp. Austin tore after her, his feet threatening to fly out from under him with every step.

"Lottie, wait!" he cried.

She turned her head to shout over her shoulder. "Don't call me that! Only Henry-James calls me that!"

Suddenly, Austin saw a thick shadow in front of her.

"Look out!" he cried.

She turned . . . and plowed into it. Both she and the dark mass tumbled to the mud, and a chorus of screams erupted.

"I caught you! I caught you!"

"Jefferson?" Austin cried.

He stumbled toward them and reached into the squirming clump of arms and legs, pulling up the first thing he touched. He held a wriggling Jefferson in midair.

"What are you *doing* here?" Austin cried.

"Looking for you—and I *caught* you!"

"And so did I."

Austin whirled around. Polly stood behind him, arms crossed over her striped cloak that trailed in the mud. He didn't have to see her mouth through the fog to know she was giving him a triumphant brown-toothed smile.

Charlotte struggled to her feet, and Austin dropped Jefferson on the ground. He gave an indignant "Hey!" and scrambled back up to plant himself in front of them both, beside Polly, as if they were cohorts.

"The poor little shaver was most upset when he woke up from his nap and found out his friends had abandoned him," Polly said, patting his shoulder. Her voice was laced with scorn. "I, of course, told him I would be glad to help him." She wrinkled her nose. "I didn't believe him when he said this was where you would be. But there were your footprints, big as life itself. Why would you come to this disgusting place?"

Charlotte stepped forward. "Why would you come? I thought Mama said you weren't to go outside."

"You weren't either! I had to come look for you so she wouldn't be upset!"

"No, you didn't! You came to *catch* me so you could take me to her—"

"Hush up!" Polly snapped. "You're jealous of me because I'm closer to Mama than you are, that's all. And with good reason. She thinks you're practically hope—"

"Charlotte has nice teeth!" Austin said.

Polly stopped in midword and stared at him, open-mouthed. Even Jefferson blinked in surprise.

"And *she's* the one who knows what's important," Austin said.

Polly recovered with a toss of her limp curls. "What do *you* know about her? *I'm* her older sister."

"And *I'm* her friend," Austin said. Charlotte wouldn't say that about *him*, not now. But he still couldn't let Charlotte hear Polly tell her that their mother thought Charlotte was hopeless.

Polly haughtily straightened her cloak.

"I'm still taking you to Mama," she said to Charlotte. Her eyes then narrowed onto Austin. "And you, too. This is just the excuse my mother needs to send you back to the North where you belong."

"No!" Jefferson shrieked. He looked up at Polly and stomped his foot. "You said nothing bad would happen if I showed you where they were!"

Polly gave him a sour smile. "I lied."

Jefferson's face collapsed, and he turned to run off down the path. Austin grabbed him and picked him up.

I'd like to run, too, he thought miserably, *but what would be the point? All Polly has to do is open her mouth and Aunt Olivia will believe her.*

Charlotte gathered her blanket and started slowly on down the path. But Polly stood staunchly in their way.

"Not so fast," she said. "I want to know one thing."

"What?" Charlotte said wearily.

"What *were* you doing out here?"

Austin glanced sharply at Jefferson. Could it be that he really hadn't told Polly about Henry-James?

Charlotte didn't say a word. Polly put her face close to her little sister's.

"You were out here looking for that slave boy, weren't you? The one Daddy said you weren't to play with anymore?"

Charlotte turned her eyes on Jefferson in fury. "You little brat!"

"You're the brat!" Polly cried. "And I know where it comes from. You've been spending too much time with this boy who believes the slaves should be able to do whatever they want to, just like free white people—this little *absolutist.*"

"You can't even say it!" Austin spat at her. "I'm an abolitionist!"

"Well, are you now?"

All four of them whipped their heads around to look down the path. Stalking toward them were two lean figures—one whose balding head shone in the light of the torch he carried, the other whose thin beard cut a scraggly silhouette in the darkness.

It was the Patty Rollers.

"Who are they?" Jefferson said. He flung his chubby arms around Austin's neck and darted his eyes suspiciously at the two men.

"Nobody," Austin said to him. "Just hush up."

"Now I wouldn't exactly call us nobody," Barnabas Brown said in his whiny voice. "We got a pretty important job to do here tonight." He squinted at Austin until his lips curled back into a yellowed smile. "And it sounds like you're just the fella to help us."

"Didn't I just hear you say you was an abolitionist?" said Irvin.

"Where are them slaves?" Barnabas said.

In Austin's arms, Jefferson stiffened, and Austin shoved his brother's head against his neck. *Please, Jefferson, be quiet—just this once.*

"Did he tell you?" Barnabas whined to Polly.

Whether she would have told him or not, Austin never knew. For from the direction of the Big House, there came a scream that cut through the night like a carving knife. Polly's head jerked toward it, and she, too, screamed.

"That's Tot!"

"That there, screechin' like a chicken?" Irvin asked.

Polly gathered up her skirts and shot off down the path, crying, "Tot! I'm coming, Tot!"

Out of the night, Tot screamed back, her voice coiling up in panic. The Patty Rollers stood there with their faces knotted in confusion. Charlotte took that opportunity to bolt after her sister. Barnabas Brown started after her, then stopped and looked back toward the swamp.

"This is the way they was comin' from," he said to Irvin. "I bet them slaves is back here!"

Austin watched in horror as they headed toward the swamp.

Henry-James, run! he wanted to scream. *They're coming!*

Throwing his head back, Austin pursed his lips and made the sound of the whippoorwill. Neither of the Patty Rollers turned to look as they rounded the bend. Austin did it again, as loud as he could, and then he took off running toward the Big House with Jefferson still hanging on like a baby possum.

The closer they got to the Big House, the clearer the voices in that direction grew.

"I'm comin', Tot!"

"Miss Polly! Help me, Miss Polly!"

As they rounded the stable, it was clear why. The door to the kitchen building was belching out flames.

Tot stood in front of it, joggling like a spring and wringing her apron in her hands. When Polly reached her, she threw her arms around Polly's neck.

"I didn't mean to! I was just warmin' the supper for Mama. I didn't mean to burn it down, Miss Polly!"

"Oh, my stars, the kitchen!" another voice cried from the back porch.

Polly stared over Tot's head, her face frozen. Austin could see the thoughts in her eyes. *"The next time she does something to endanger the welfare of this household, she is gone."*

"Josephine!" Aunt Olivia was shouting. "Mousie! Isaac! Where is everyone?"

Her voice drew closer. In Polly's arms, Tot moaned, and Polly didn't seem able to move at all.

Do something! Austin wanted to shout at her. *Don't let Aunt Olivia catch her!*

"Polly!" he hissed instead. "She's coming!"

Polly looked at him wildly.

"Someone get some water!" Aunt Olivia was crying—from just the other side of the kitchen. Austin pulled Jefferson off him and shoved him toward Charlotte. "Take him!" he whispered.

Then he turned to Tot and Polly, still stuck together.

"Tot!" Austin whispered hoarsely. "Run! Hide someplace where no one will think to look for you!"

She rolled her black eyes up at Polly until they shone in the firelight.

"Yes, go!" Polly hissed.

Tot plodded heavily off into the darkness, still sniveling loudly.

"You run, too, Polly, into the house!" Austin whispered. "And don't tell anyone you saw her here!"

Polly's eyes darted to his. "Why? So *you* can tell? Make my daddy think you're his big helper?"

Austin shook his head frantically as he pushed her toward the house. "No, we'll keep your secret if you'll keep ours."

Her lip started to curl, but Austin kept pushing and said, "Do you want your best friend to be sold?"

Her muddy brown eyes met his, and she shook her head.

"Then go!" he whispered. "Run!"

She did then, tearing around one side of the burning building just as her mother appeared on the other side. Aunt Olivia gaped up at her kitchen and pressed the sides of her head with her hands.

"Where *is* everyone?" she cried. "Will no one put this out?"

"I'll get help!" Austin called to her.

Aunt Olivia snapped her head around.

"You!" she shrieked.

"I'm going to get some men—"

"No!" She moved toward him like an angry spirit through the night. "You started this fire, and by heaven, you'll put it out!"

✦ ✦ ✦

Chapter Eighteen

ustin stared. "You think *I* started the fire?"

"I don't see anyone else here, do you?" said Aunt Olivia.

Austin looked around at the yard, now clouded with smoke. His heart began to pound. Except for the inky figures just emerging from the stable area, there was no one.

"It wasn't me!" Austin said.

"Who was it then?"

Smoke stung his eyes, and he squeezed them shut. *If I tell, then Polly will tell—*

"Missus, we got some buckets here!" Isaac called out from behind them.

"Where have you been? Get this fire out before it catches the house!"

Aunt Olivia drew her shawl around her and hurried into the stream of slaves who ran up from the stable with wooden buckets sloshing water. Her orders barked out above the crackling of the flames that were slowly turning the kitchen building into a blackened cave.

Austin peered through the smoke toward the house.

The back door opened and Kady floated billowing skirts down the steps.

Kady . . . who doesn't trust me either, Austin thought.

He backed away from the building and hurried to the end of the line of slaves. Someone handed him a heavy bucket, and he turned to place it into a pair of black hands. Austin saw that they belonged to Henry-James.

The Patty Rollers didn't catch you! Austin started to say.

But Henry-James grunted at him as he took the bucket and passed it off. "What you doin' here?" he said. "Ain't you done enough?"

Austin couldn't answer. His throat was closed up.

"Go on now, we don't need you," Henry-James said.

"You hush up, Henry-James," said a quiet voice. "We need all the help we can get."

Henry-James scowled and moved up the line. Stepping between them, Kady took the bucket Austin handed her and passed it on to Henry-James.

"Mama says you started the fire, Austin," she said. She gave the startled Henry-James a nudge. "Just you keep working."

"I didn't," Austin said.

"I know."

Austin looked at her quickly, his eyes still stinging.

"But if you'll tell me who did, I'll help you," Kady said.

No, you won't! No one here will! I try and I try to be their friends, and they still don't trust me!

Kady's eyebrows shot up to her hairline, and Henry-James's chin fell to his chest—and Austin realized he hadn't just thought it. He'd said it.

He dropped his bucket and ran—away from the Big House and the burning kitchen and the startled cries of "Austin, come back!" Away from the place where he'd wanted to fit in—and where he just didn't.

He ran, feet slithering over the mud, and leaned on the first thing he could find—Daddy Elias's fence.

They don't want me here, *that's for sure,* he thought. He gasped in a few more breaths and turned to leave.

"Where you off to, Massa Austin?" a voice said from the porch.

Austin looked through the wisps of smoke that had escaped to Slave Street. "I don't know, Daddy Elias," he said.

"Then I reckon you right where you s'pose to be already."

There wasn't anyplace else to go. Austin trudged wearily inside the gate and up to the porch. He followed Daddy Elias into the warm cabin, where the only smoke came from his tiny fire.

Daddy Elias sank down into his rocker and motioned for Austin to sit on the floor at his feet. Quietly, he began to talk.

"Now, You knows our Massa Austin be confused and he don't know which way for to turn. I tol' him and tol' him You his friend and You gon' help him if'n he just ask You—"

Austin looked up at the old man with a start. His eyes were softly crinkled shut and his snowy head was bowed.

He's praying! Austin thought. In spite of himself, he looked around the room and half expected to see the man Jesus standing right there. He didn't see Him—but he felt Him, just the way he had down by the swamp.

"So I reckon I gon' have to bring him to You myself. You see this here boy, Lord? He think he don't fit, and I reckon he's right. This boy smart—he *know* he ain't like folks here. He got

book-learnin' and he got things in his head his daddy teach him
that don't nobody 'round here even think about. He all tore up
'bout that, Jesus, and You know he don't need to be 'cause
them folks that's different—them's the ones You say, 'C'mon
here, boy—you follow Me now'. He don't know yet 'bout bein'
different is *how* he fit. You needs all them different pieces for to
make this big ol' world we's all a part of. Now, Jesus—he need
You for to teach him that. And Lordy, I knows You can."

He breathed an "Ay-Men," and the cabin was quiet.

"You think He heard that?" Austin whispered.

"He always hear," Daddy Elias said. "Trouble is, we folks
here, we don't always be listenin' when He answer."

The questions swirled in Austin's head, but he didn't ask
any of them. He closed his eyes and tried to listen.

What he heard was the gate squeaking open, and a pair
of bare feet slapping across the cold porch. The door pushed
in, and Henry-James said, "I knew you'd be here—"

"I'm sorry!" Austin said. "Daddy Elias told me to come in."

"Well, come on," Henry-James said. "Miss Polly out here,
and she need to talk to you—bad!" Henry-James grabbed him
by the elbow and dragged him out the door.

Sure enough, Polly was standing outside the gate,
shivering and crying tears that stuck straggly strands of her
hair right to her cheeks. Beside her sat Bogie, growling
doubtfully under his breath. Polly cowered away from him,
but when she saw Austin, she cried, "Thank heaven!"

"For what?" Austin said.

"You told Tot to run," Polly said, "and she's run off for
good, I think. She hasn't come back yet!"

"She prob'ly 'fraid she gon' get whupped," Henry-James said.

"She will, or worse, if she doesn't come back before

Mama discovers she's gone!" Polly said.

Austin sighed heavily. He was getting used to being blamed for things. "I'm sorry," he said. "I just wanted her to get out of sight so your mother wouldn't blame her for the fire."

"So then she blame Massa Austin!" Henry-James said bitterly.

Austin looked at him in surprise.

"Please find her for me!" Polly said. "I'm not blaming you, honest. I just want her back! If you don't find her and Daddy does, he'll sell her!"

"No, he won't," Austin said. "Uncle Drayton wouldn't do that. Aunt Olivia was just trying to scare you."

But both Henry-James and Polly shook their heads, and Polly started on a fresh bout of tears.

"*Please*, Austin!" she said.

Don't you mean Boston *Austin?* he thought. But another thought chased that one out. *If I had a friend like that, I'd do everything to help her, too. But I don't know how! I'm the outsider here. So why is she coming to me?*

From the porch there was a cough, and Austin looked up to see Daddy Elias there, still wrapped in his quilt against the damp air, watching Austin through the wispy smoke. *"Jesus, we be friends,"* he'd said. *"You show me the way."*

"All right," Austin said. "Where do you think she would go?"

"I don't know! She never goes anywhere unless I tell her to!"

Henry-James touched his elbow. "I reckon Bogie, he could find her," he said. "If'n you wants my help," he added.

Austin only nodded. He was too surprised to speak.

"You got something with you smells like Tot?" Henry-James asked Polly.

Polly looked down at herself helplessly. "No," she said.

Austin shook himself out of his shock and felt a grin quiver across his face. "The way Tot is always hanging on you, I bet the clothes you have on smell just like her!"

Polly only thought about that for a moment before she untied her striped satin cape. "Here," she said.

"Will he be confused between Polly's scent and Tot's?" Austin asked.

"Bogie, he a smart dog," Henry-James said. "You jus' watch."

Austin and Polly did, as Henry-James held the cape down in front of Bogie's nose. The skin smoothed out over the dog's wrinkled forehead as his nostrils trembled over it. He turned his head at once toward Polly and gave her a sniff. Then he took another snort at the cape and began to snuffle the ground. He looked up at Henry-James, ears dangling.

"He don't smell nothin' of her here," Henry-James said, handing her back the cape. "He sayin' we got to keep lookin'."

"But he's got the scent?" Austin said.

"Yep."

"All right, Polly," Austin said. His mind was spinning as if it had wheels. "What did you tell her when she left?"

"*You* told her to go someplace where no one would think to look for her."

"Did you ever tell her *not* to go somewhere?"

Polly gave her head a frenzied shake. "She just goes along with me—except tonight she wouldn't—when I told her I was going to the swamp. She said she'd rather work in the kitchen—which she hates—than go to that old place."

"Let's go," Henry-James said.

By now the drizzling rain had stopped and the clouds were blowing past the moon, giving the night a cool light to show their way. Just ahead of him, Austin could see

Henry-James and the loudly sniffing Bogie, and at his side he felt Polly clinging to his sleeve. Austin had long since dropped his horse blanket, but even in the chilly dampness, he had too many other things to think about.

He was busy dragging a branch behind them, for one thing. And he was scouring the woods on both sides of the path with his eyes, looking for flashes of Tot's apron. Mostly he was waiting for Bogie's tail to wag purposefully.

They were halfway down the path to the swamp, and there was still no sign of her. Polly was starting to whimper.

"Don't worry," Austin said to her. "Henry-James and Bogie can do just about anything."

"How do you know that for sure?" she said pitifully. "Are you friends?"

Austin wanted to say yes. *But I can't,* he thought. *I thought I could, but I can't.*

And maybe it didn't matter now anyway. It was certain Aunt Olivia wanted to believe he'd burned down the kitchen. He and Mother and Jefferson would be headed north.

"What is it, boy?" Henry-James said suddenly.

Bogie's growl worked its way into a howl with his head thrown back and his brown-furred skin quivering with excitement. With his head pointed to the ground like a finger, he followed it swiftly down the path.

"Looka here!" Henry-James whispered. "We got us some footprints."

Austin hurried to join him, with Polly's fingers still curled around his sleeve.

"Couldn't those be the Patty Rollers, though?" Austin said as he peered at the boot-shaped imprints in the mud.

"These here is," Henry-James said, pointing to one set.

"But Tot, she barefooted. And see . . ." He crept along beside the other, toed prints. "They come out of the woods right here, and they be from the walk of somebody mighty clumsy."

"There goes Bogie!" Austin said.

Bogie had already turned the next curve in the path, sniffing so loudly they could still hear him. The three of them bolted after him, with Henry-James holding his hand out so they didn't get too close.

Austin continued to drag the branch behind him. His ears pounded with Daddy Elias's words: "*Jesus, we be friends. You show me the way.*"

Suddenly, Bogie howled again, but Austin heard a moan as well.

"That's Tot!" Polly cried.

She let go of Austin's sleeve and pushed past Henry-James. But when she got to Bogie, he grabbed at her skirt with his teeth and hung on.

"Let me go, you . . . dog!" she whispered hoarsely.

"Somethin' wrong," Henry-James murmured to Austin. "C'mon with me."

Heart hammering near his throat, Austin followed Henry-James, while Bogie kept Polly out of sight. Just around the curve, at the edge of the swamp, they both stopped. They could see through the leaves that on either side of Tot stood the Patty Rollers.

Henry-James started to leap forward, but Austin pulled him back into the brush. He felt something slash at his right arm as he pulled Henry-James's ear close to his mouth.

"You can't let them see you!" he whispered. "You don't have a pass! Take Polly and get help!"

"How *you* gonna get Tot loose?" Henry-James hissed.

Austin had no idea, but he gave him a push. "I always think of something."

"This ain't one of your adventures, Massa Austin!"

"Sure it is. Now go on before *you* get caught!"

Henry-James reluctantly slipped out of the bushes.

"What was that?" a whiny voice on the other side of the brush said.

"It was me!" Austin cried—in his best South Carolina accent.

He burst out onto the edge of the swamp and marched up to Tot, careful to keep his face toward the ground. *"This ain't one of your adventures,"* Henry-James had said. *But I'm just going to pretend it is.*

"Thank heavens you caught her," he said gruffly to the ground. "I've been looking for this slave half the night."

"Massa Austin!" Tot cried in her fingernail-scraping voice.

"Thank you, gentlemen," Austin said. "I will see that my uncle pays you well. Now if you'll turn her over to me. . . ."

Tot was so confused that her mouth went slack. Even Irvin and Barnabas stood squinting at him for a moment, both sets of lips curled back in yellow-toothed befuddlement.

"Come on with me, you little cuffee!" Austin said.

"You sure we're gonna get paid?" Barnabas whined.

"Of course! My uncle is a man of his word."

Barnabas let go of Tot on one side, and Austin tried not to puff out a sigh of relief. But Irvin held fast.

"Wait just a minute," he growled. "Ain't you the same one that little missy told us was a abolitionist?"

Austin forced a laugh. "Me? Heavens no! I'd skin the hide of any absolutist I ran into. You see, I can't even say it!"

Irvin pulled Tot up to his face by both arms. "Is this here boy your master?" he snarled.

She gave a heartbreaking moan.

"I'm not her master!" Austin cried. "My uncle is her master, but I know my responsibilities, living in his house. Let go of her at once, or you'll have to answer to him!"

But Barnabas seized both of his arms from behind and wrenched them backward. His fingers dug hard into Austin's right arm, and a startling pain pushed a yelp out of Austin.

"Quit your whinin' and snivelin'!" Barnabas jeered. "Are you a sissy?"

The words shot through Austin like a bullet. "No, I'm *not!* I may not be a big, *mean* man like you, but I'm—"

"What?" Irvin said with a hard laugh. *"What* are ya—sissy Yankee boy?"

Austin's head clouded. *I'm . . . different. I'm just different. How is that going to get us out of here?*

And then as if he were standing right there, Austin heard Daddy Elias's voice. *"Bein' different is* how *you fit."*

Austin drew himself up and looked Irvin Ullmann full in the face.

"That's him, all right!" Irvin cried. "The dirty little abolitionist!"

"Actually," Austin said in his best Baltimore voice, "they call me Boston Austin—because I'm so smart."

He felt Barnabas shake with a guffaw. "Is that a fact?"

"It is. I've *forgotten* more about slavery than you will ever know. Did you know that Nat Turner was born the year of the Gabriel Prosser uprising—1800—and that he died in 1831, the same year Tice Davids vanished and his master gave the Underground Railroad its name?"

"Huh?" Barnabas said.

"I think if you're going to patrol the slaves you ought to

at least know what you're talking about!" Austin said. "Haven't you read William Garrison's antislavery newspaper, *The Liberator?* Did you know that although 55 whites were killed in the Nat Turner Rebellion, 120 black lives were lost—in just one day?"

"Served them right!" Barnabas cried and squeezed his arms harder.

But Austin saw the confusion flicker in Irvin's eyes and he pushed on, lowering his voice dramatically, the way Reverend Pullens did in church.

"Of course you would say that, because you've never thought about this: Slavery has become so necessary here that it has ceased to appear evil to you." He pulled forward, tugging Barnabas with him. "But it appears evil to Jesus. Did you know that?"

Irvin stared at him as Austin waited for an answer, just the way Daddy Elias did when he was telling a story in the cabin. As he watched the balding man's face, he caught a movement out of the corner of his eye. In the moonlight, he saw something white across the swamp, between the cypress trees. No, *two* something whites. He kept his eyes on Irvin so he, too, wouldn't turn around and look. The wheels in Austin's head spun like one of Jefferson's tops.

Something white across the swamp—Brawley and Seton again? The ghost of a slave come to haunt the Patty Rollers? Someone *playing* at ghosts?

And then Austin knew. Trying not to grin, he raised his voice and charged on.

"Let me tell you the story of the Nat Turner Rebellion!" he said loudly. "You may think the slave owners won, but I want you to hear about the courage, the determination, of those slaves to take the freedom the good Lord wants them to have!"

"He does talk like one of them Boston professors!" Barnabas said behind him.

Tot was staring at him, her eyes wide with fear and amazement, and even Irvin stiffened. Beyond them all, Austin could see the two white things moving closer. He wasn't sure, but he thought he heard a low and eerie wail. He lowered his own voice a little.

"William Garrison wrote, 'That which is not just is not law'!" Austin said. "'Let southern oppressors tremble. Let all the enemies of the persecuted blacks tremble—'"

"Woooo!"

Barnabas jerked, and Irvin snapped his head around.

"What was that?" he said.

As they searched the swamp with their startled gazes, Austin caught Tot's eyes. "It's all right," he mouthed. She pressed her lips together.

"Nat Turner never read the words of William Lloyd Garrison," Austin said, suddenly wishing he could wave a fist for drama, "but he believed God had placed him on earth to help free the slaves from their oppression—"

"Hush up!" Irvin hissed. He jerked his head at Barnabas, and Barnabas let go of Austin's arms and moved to the edge of the swamp. Austin didn't move yet.

"Woooo!" came the chilling wail from out of the swampy mist.

And then there was a flash of white—and then another.

"Ghost!" Barnabas cried.

"Don't be a fool, ya nincompoop!" said Irvin.

But he, too, let go of Tot and edged closer. Austin held up a hand to Tot, and she squeezed her face in tight.

"Woooo! Woooo!" came again—with a great rattling of pampas grass and cypress limbs.

"It *is* ghosts!" Barnabas whined. "It's the ghosts of them slaves—and I ain't staying."

"Woooo!"

"Go, Tot!" Austin hissed.

She did, careening across the mud, unnoticed by the Patty Rollers. Austin, too, began to back up. *Just one more wooo, and I can be gone.*

The white figures moved mysteriously through the trees, closer and closer. Barnabas gave a final wail and, turning on the heel of his boot, flew past Austin and down the path away from the swamp. Irvin, however, was not so easily moved. Although Austin saw the man's pant legs quiver, Ullmann stood stock-still and peered.

"Them ain't no ghosts," he whispered. "I think them are petticoats."

He whirled to look at Austin, anger sparking from his eyes. And then, from beyond the cypress knees, there was a howl so harrowing that even Austin caught his breath.

Irvin Ullmann came up on his toes as if he'd been shot in the behind. With a terrified yowl, he spun around and tore from the swamp like a bewildered turkey. Austin had to cover his mouth with his hands.

"You got them!" he hissed across the swamp.

But the *wooing* continued, and two white figures, clad from head to toe in white petticoats and bed sheets, wove their way among the cypress trees and off into the woods toward the Big House. Austin chuckled and took off down the path. He could hear the "ghosts" crackling amid the underbrush as they ran through the woods alongside him, with Bogie still howling. Ahead, Irvin was still running and screaming.

As he rounded the bend in the path, Austin saw the white figures drawing closer. The shorter one burst from the woods and ran toward him, and Austin could hear her giggling under her disguise.

"Good job!" Austin whispered to her. "Where's Henry-James going?"

Charlotte stopped and looked ahead. Henry-James had come out of the woods, too, but he was heading on down the path, sheet trailing out behind him. "Woooooo!" he howled.

Bogie crashed from the bushes, baying plaintively, and followed him.

"That's enough, Henry-James," Austin whispered as loudly as he dared.

But Henry-James kept on, gaining inch by inch on the fleeing Irvin Ullmann.

"Woooooo—Patty Roller!" he wailed, and Bogie howled.

Irvin twisted a terrified face toward him, and Henry-James dodged toward the edge of the path. Irvin turned back around and kept on going—but Austin and Charlotte both watched in horror.

Just as Irvin turned his head, Henry-James's sheet caught on a bush. In one step, it ripped off and dangled there.

✟ ⊹ ✟

Chapter Nineteen

ogie stopped in his tracks and cocked his baggy head. Irvin Ullmann turned around once more, and Henry-James took off for the woods.

But Irvin Ullmann scrambled after him and dove, grabbing on to his legs and writhing with him to the ground.

"I got you now, you little thievin' cuffee!" Irvin growled.

He pulled himself up on Henry-James, who didn't make a sound.

But Bogie did.

Growling ferociously, Bogie hurled himself at the Patty Roller and dug in with all four paws. He sank his teeth firmly into the seat of Irvin Ullmann's pants, and he didn't let go.

Irvin yipped like a dog himself and rolled away.

Henry-James scrambled up from the ground and looked wildly from left to right.

"Let's go!" Austin cried. He grabbed Charlotte by the hand and gave Henry-James a shove. They took off down the path with Bogie still snarling and Irvin still shrieking.

Austin felt the cold air on his teeth as he grinned. "We did it!" he cried.

And then they rounded the bend—straight into the arms of Barnabas Brown. He stuck out his hands and grabbed, catching Austin and Henry-James by their shirtfronts.

"Go, Miss Lottie!" Henry-James yelled.

"Get help!" Austin cried.

"Ain't no help for you now," Barnabas said as Charlotte's footsteps disappeared frantically down the path. "You done used up all your tricks on me."

Austin's mind raced once more. "You've made a mistake!" he said to Barnabas. "Show him your pass, Henry-James."

Henry-James turned his head to look blankly at Austin.

"You didn't lose it, did you?" Austin said tightly.

Light dawned in Henry-James's eyes and he said, with exaggerated mourning, "Yes, Massa Austin."

"You can't trust one of them," Austin said to Barnabas. But Barnabas dragged them both back up the path.

As they rounded the curve, Austin expected to see Irvin a mass of bloody flesh. But although Bogie was still on top of him, snarling and pulling at his clothes with his teeth, Irvin's only injury seemed to be a throat hoarse from shrieking.

"Now, you get that miserable cur off Irvin!" Barnabas cried.

"Don't do it, Henry-James!" Austin said. "He can't do anything to us!"

As if in answer, Barnabas flung both of them to the ground, so hard it knocked the breath out of Austin. With his foot firmly planted on Henry-James's back, Barnabas reached inside his own jacket and pulled out something metallic and shiny. He pointed it at Bogie.

"The gun!" Austin said. "He's going to shoot Bogie!"

"No!" Henry-James screamed. "Bogie, turn him loose, boy!"

His teeth still embedded in Irvin's pants, Bogie stopped growling and rolled his eyes toward Henry-James.

"Turn him loose!" Henry-James cried.

As if he hated to do it, Bogie let go. He lifted his lips once more at Irvin and then trotted dutifully over to Henry-James, snarling at the foot on his back. Barnabas slid it off quickly, but he leaned over and plucked Henry-James up by the back of his shirt. Irvin rose from the ground and yanked Austin up. For the first time that night, real anxiety raced through Austin. Barnabas was right. He was out of tricks. He could only think, *"Jesus, we be friends. You show me the way."*

"Henry-James Ravenal!" said a shrill voice behind them. "You would lose your little black head if it weren't attached."

Austin gazed at Polly, marching down the path toward them. She was still dressed in her now muddied striped satin cape. Her eyes were so red and puffy that Austin could hardly see them. She held out a white piece of paper.

"You must have dropped this pass before you even left the house, Henry-James," she said.

"Let me see that," Irvin growled. He let go of Austin with one hand to snatch the paper from Polly.

He read the paper, his lips moving silently.

"What's it say?" Barnabas said.

"This here's a pass all right," Irvin said. "Signed by Mr. Ravenal." He shoved the paper back toward Polly. "But it's a fake. First place, ain't nobody gonna let a slave go traipsin' around the swamp at night, and second place, Mr. Ravenal ain't even here! He's over in St. Stephen's Parish lookin' for that other lyin', thievin' cuffee!"

"You are as stupid as you look," Polly said calmly. "My

father is in his library right this very minute!"

Austin's eyes popped. *Polly must have a lot of practice,* he thought. *She sure can lie and make it sound like the truth.*

"Is that so?" Irvin said. He took hold of Austin's other arm, squeezing it painfully with his fingers. "Then I reckon we better take this boy to him and tell him what his nephew has been up to this evening."

"Oh, I don't advise that," Polly said. "When he finds out what you've done to his nephew, you'll probably both be put in jail. Austin is, after all, the apple of my father's eye."

Barnabas looked at Austin doubtfully. "He does look like a Ravenal."

"I know he has it in mind to turn some of the running of the plantation over to him very soon." Polly ran her eyes over Austin and let her mouth grow stern. "Look at that," she said. "You've even made him bleed. That is sure to get you in some very big trouble."

They all followed her gaze to Austin's left arm. Austin himself bit back a gasp. His shirtsleeve was soaked in crimson. Irvin let go and looked at his red palm. His face stiffened.

"Do you want to go to my father with his nephew's blood on your hands?" Polly said. "If you do, you'll never get another dime from him."

Irvin didn't even give it a second thought. "C'mon," he said tightly to Barnabas. "Let's get on home."

Barnabas seemed more than eager to go. He dropped Henry-James and edged on down the path. Irvin started to follow him, giving Bogie a wide berth. But just as he turned to leave, he stopped, and his eyes glittered on Henry-James. Like a swinging ax, Irvin lunged toward him and savagely pulled him up to his twisted yellow mouth.

"You watch yourself, cuffee!" he said viciously. "If I ever catch you off Canaan Grove without a pass, I will beat you to within an inch of your sorry life *before* I turn you in."

The look in Henry-James's eyes froze Austin from heart to toe. It was a look he'd seen only once before—not so long ago, in the train yard. That slave on the ground who had just been kicked in the side, and knew worse was coming to him, had looked just that way. It was a look he'd never seen on Henry-James before.

Then the Patty Roller shoved him away and disappeared up the path. Austin stayed cold with fear until his footsteps faded away.

"You have to stay away from him," Austin said. "We're going to walk you home in case he tries anything—"

"We don't have time!" Polly said, plucking at his sleeve. "We have to get home before Daddy discovers we're gone."

"He really is home?" Austin said.

"Yes," she said. "I don't lie about *everything*. I only lie when I have to." She gave him a tug. "Come on!"

Austin turned to Henry-James, but he and Bogie had already slipped soundlessly away.

Austin and Polly were somewhat louder as they made their way toward the Big House.

"What happened to Charlotte?" Austin asked.

"I got her in the back door while Daddy and Mama were in the library. She told me what was happening. I knew the only thing to do was to bring you a pass."

"How did you get it?"

"I wrote it myself, silly," she said. "Daddy's signature is easy to copy."

"What about Tot?"

"Scared half out of her mind. She's under my bed—and Charlotte better have my sheets back on it by now."

"One sheet is still on a branch back there," Austin said.

"That's all right," Polly said. "That one was Kady's."

"But won't Kady tell?"

"She would never tell on her precious Charlotte, no matter what she did," Polly said.

Austin thought he heard hurt in her voice.

I know how that feels, he thought sadly. *Everyone has their friendships safe again—except me.*

That brought him to one more question, one he was almost afraid to ask. But the Big House was in sight, and if he didn't ask now, he knew he would probably never have another chance.

"What you said about Uncle Drayton," Austin said slowly, "about me being 'the apple of his eye.' Was that true?"

Polly shrugged her narrow shoulders. "I made it up just to get rid of those awful Patty Rollers."

"Oh," Austin said.

She pointed toward the Big House, now only a few steps away. "Daddy!" she whispered. "He's in the back hall!"

She was right. Several lamps flickered near the back door, and Drayton Ravenal passed in their light.

Austin motioned Polly behind the big live oak and they peered around it, waiting.

Uncle Drayton hovered, first at one window, then at the other. Finally, he busied himself at the door, and then disappeared toward the front of the house.

To Austin's surprise, Polly grabbed his hand. Hers felt frail and tiny—not at all like a bird's claw would. Together they dodged in and out of the shadows and crept quietly up the back steps. But when Polly tried to push the back door open, it wouldn't budge.

"He's bolted it!" she whispered. "We'll have to try the front door."

But a panicked scurry around the Big House to the front revealed the same thing—that one was locked, too, and they saw the library door open. Austin ducked and pulled Polly down with him.

"Your father!" he mouthed to her.

She nodded and crawled to the edge of the porch with Austin behind her. They both jumped off and inched their way along the side of the house.

"What are we going to do?" Polly said.

Austin closed his eyes to think, but nothing would come to him. *I really have used up all my tricks.*

"Maybe we should just knock on the door and have Uncle Drayton let us in," Austin said.

Polly's eyes swelled. "We can't! We'd have to tell him the whole story—" Her voice caught. "You have never seen my father when he's angry—and you don't want to."

"We're not his slaves!" Austin cried. "He wouldn't treat us the way he treats them!"

And then suddenly, he knew it was true—and that he'd known it all along. Uncle Drayton did mistreat his slaves. The knowledge weighed on Austin like a heavy hand—because it meant he *had* to think of one more trick.

"All right," he said to Polly. "Come on."

He grabbed her wrist and pulled her with him to a big poplar at the side of the house. As Polly hid behind it, Austin pulled his head back and, cupping his hands around his mouth, made the sound of a whippoorwill.

Once, twice, and a third time he called.

"Come on, Charlotte," he whispered. "Answer just once more."

And then, as if she'd heard his words, a window on the second story slid open, and a small head came out. It gave a whippoorwill's answering call, and Austin stepped away from the tree and waved. Charlotte waved back and then disappeared inside. Polly shivered at Austin's side, but Austin wasn't scared now.

"Just wait," he said. "Something will happen."

Sure enough, Charlotte's silhouette appeared in the window again, and with her another, taller one.

"Kady!" Polly whispered.

Austin watched as they seemed to be tying something together. Charlotte then looked out and waved again, and Austin caught Polly's elbow.

They ran, bent low, across the yard to the side of the house. Dangling above them was a sheet.

Kady hissed down to them, "Grab on, and we'll pull you up!"

"It's me, Polly," she said.

"I know," Kady whispered back impatiently. "Come on!"

For the first time that night, maybe for the first time ever, Austin saw Polly give a real smile as she grabbed on to the sheet and her feet left the ground.

He was halfway up the side of the house himself when he realized that her teeth hadn't even seemed brown.

☦-☦-☦

Chapter Twenty

"When the Patty Rollers finally let us go, there was Uncle Drayton in the hallway."

"And that's why Kady and Charlotte had to sneak you in through my window." Sally Hutchinson nodded toward the two bodies curled up in the chairs in front of her fireplace. She ran her hand over Austin's hair. "You should be asleep, too."

Austin shook his head. "I can't. Daddy Elias says I look like I have puzzle pieces rattling around in my head, and that's how it feels."

"I always loved that old man, too." His mother smiled faintly.

"You knew him!" Austin said.

"I always played with his daughter. My mama thought she would become my 'girl,' but I was like Kady. I didn't want a slave of my own." Her voice was suddenly sad. "I thought Ria and I could still be friends, but when she turned 13 and they put her to work, my father forbade it. I tried to see her anyway—"

"Ria!" Austin cried. "She's Henry-James's mother!"

"She's still here?" Mother said. Her eyes grew glossy. "My sweet Ria."

"She's still here," Austin said, "but she doesn't like me.

"Ria was always very cautious. But you give her time—she'll come around." She sighed. "I would love to see her."

They were quiet for a minute.

"I can almost *hear* the questions in your head," Mother said. She gave his hand a squeeze. "Don't you think it's better when you ask them out loud?"

"I've had to tell so many lies!"

She tilted her fawn-colored head. "You've *had* to?"

"That's the way Polly said it. She only lies when she has to."

"Why does she have to?"

"Because she wants to keep Tot."

"And why did you 'have to' lie?"

The answers pushed their way into his head like a bewildered mob of sheep. "So Charlotte and Henry-James could still be friends—"

"Even though her father forbade it."

"But he was wrong!" Austin said.

"Is that the only reason?"

Austin looked down at the covers. "I wanted them for my friends, too. I thought if I helped them, I would . . . fit."

"And then what happened?"

"One lie just made me have to tell one more—or at least not tell the truth. But don't you see? If we had told the truth, Uncle Drayton would have whipped Henry-James and sold Tot. The Patty Rollers would have found all the slaves. Don't you think they're wrong?"

"I do," she said softly. "But I don't let it force me to do

other things I know are just as wrong." She took Austin's hand between both of hers. "Your father told you, 'Slavery has become so necessary here that it has ceased to appear evil.' Think about it. What has become so necessary to you that it has stopped seeming wrong?"

"Lying." His chest pinched. "And teaching Jefferson to lie."

"Ah."

"But you don't tell Uncle Drayton the truth!"

His mother's eyebrows went up on her pale face. "He knows exactly how I feel about slavery. He knows that I will not keep my mouth shut about it around here. Aunt Olivia has already had a hissy fit because I talk to Kady about my opinions."

"But Uncle Drayton can't tell you who you can be friends with!"

"He can't tell you either," she said. "And if you had just come to me, I would have settled it."

Austin stared at her. "But I thought you loved Uncle Drayton."

"I do, and he loves me. That doesn't mean we always have to agree. And how is he ever going to see our side if we don't tell him?"

Austin sat up, wriggling anxiously. "But Polly told me to keep my mouth shut about being an abolitionist."

Mother laughed a jingly laugh. "Is Polly the person you most want to please?"

Austin felt his face flushing. "No, I just wanted her to like me. I want everyone to like me."

"Ah," she said, smiling wryly. "I would love for Aunt Olivia to like me, but as long as I stand for abolition, that isn't going to happen. Which one do I give up?"

"But I don't want to give up Charlotte, or Henry-James, if they'll still have me."

"I'm certain they will," Mother said. "But I think you have to start with the truth. If you take your other friend with you, I think you'll be surprised."

"What other friend? You mean Jesus?" Austin said.

"That's who I mean."

"Do you think we can find out from Him why He lets Daddy Elias and Henry-James and the rest of them be slaves, if He loves them so much?"

Mother closed her eyes and smiled. "Oh, Austin, when I shut my eyes, I think it's Wesley I hear when you talk." But she opened them again, and she grinned. "Do you realize that it's the Hutchinson in you that helped you out of trouble with the Patty Rollers last night—lecturing them to distract them from the 'ghosts'?"

"Is that anything like 'being different is *how* I fit'?"

"Now *that* sounds like Elias to me!" Mother said, laughing. "Enough questions. I think it's time you got some sleep. It's nearly dawn."

Austin did feel drowsy, and he slid down on the pillows and turned over. His arm protested with an angry sting.

"Ow!"

"What? That cut on your arm?"

"It hurts."

She frowned. "Most planters' wives are good nurses, but that isn't Aunt Olivia's talent, as I've found out. I wonder who—?"

"I know someone," said a groggy voice from the chair. Kady sat up, dark hair falling down in wisps. "I'll go fetch her soon as it's light."

At least, that was what Austin *thought* she said. He drifted off to sleep before the last syllable was out.

"Mmmm-mmmm, Miz Sally, he's got hisself tangled up with some pampas grass. You raised you a Yankee child, sure enough."

Austin opened his eyes to catch a foggy view of Ria, bent over his arm with a bandage and a bowl of water.

"I know about pampas grass," he said sleepily. "If you run through it, it can cut you up."

The next time Austin opened his eyes, he could hear Mother's and Ria's voices humming near the fireplace. Someone else was beside his bed. He tried to focus on the miles of green ribbon that went around her skirt.

"We still have a secret agreement, right?" Polly whispered.

"I'm going to tell Uncle Drayton I'm friends with Henry-James myself," Austin whispered back. He licked his dry lips. "I'm tired of lying, aren't you?"

"Go back to Boston, Austin," she said tightly. "You don't know how it is here."

She went off in a swish of green satin.

So far this isn't working very well, he thought. He began to doze away again.

"Where are we going to play today, Austin?"

Austin pried his eyes open to see Jefferson bounding across the bed. The sun was now streaming in through the drapes.

"We're not playing today, shrimp," Austin said. "Not until I talk to Uncle Drayton."

Jefferson's eyes grew saucer wide. "Are you going to *tell?*"

Austin nodded. "And there isn't going to be any more lying, so it doesn't matter now that you told Kady where

Henry-James was and you told Polly we were with him."

"I did not either tell Polly! I told her where *you* were because I wanted to help!"

"Jefferson, honey," said a voice from the doorway. "Why don't you go get Austin another pillow?" Kady crossed to the bed, looking crisp and tidied up.

Jefferson scampered off, and Kady took his place on the edge of the bed. "Jefferson never said a word to me about Henry-James. I already knew that. That's why I got the play place out of Jefferson, so I could go there and warn Henry-James about the Patty Rollers and tell him Seton had escaped."

Austin's head was whirling. "How did you know about Henry-James?"

"Charlotte told me. We tell each other everything. She's the only one I can trust around here."

Austin's chest pinched. "I know," he said. "She told me you didn't trust *me.*"

Kady shook her head. "Only on that day with the Patty Rollers when you told them you hoped 'that little cuffee' got caught!"

"I was pretending!"

"I know that now. When Charlotte told me you were going to help her and Henry-James, I knew you were on our side."

"'Our side'?" Austin said. "Are you—?"

"Don't ask that yet, Austin," Kady said. "I'm still trying to decide. Now, are you going to come back to lessons with Charlotte and me?"

She grinned at him and went toward the door. Jefferson barreled in across her path, tossed the pillow on top of

Austin's covers, and bolted after her.

"Are you going to play with me today?" he said.

"Of course," Kady said.

The door had barely closed behind her when it opened again, and a box-shaped head poked in.

"Boy, what are you doin' up here in the Big House!" Ria cried.

Henry-James slid in, shutting the door behind him as if he were still dodging the Patty Rollers. "Daddy 'Lias sent me with this here boneset tea. He say Massa Austin want it for Miz Sally."

"You must be Henry-James," Austin's mother said.

She extended her hand gracefully to Henry-James, and Austin watched in amusement as he shuffled over to her and stuck his own chocolate-colored paw into it, head bobbing awkwardly.

"I've heard so much about you," Mother said.

"You can go on home now," Ria said.

"Oh, no, Ria, please let him stay a minute," Mother said. "I'm sure he and Austin have a lot to talk about."

Henry-James hurried over to Austin, looking out of place amid the brocades and porcelains.

"Where's Bogie?" Austin whispered.

"He standin' by the back porch, just a-growlin' under his breath 'cause he can't come in." Henry-James looked around uneasily again. "I got to tell you, Massa Austin, I was wrong 'bout you."

Austin's heart got heavy. "I know. You thought I was smart, but I almost led the Patty Rollers right to you."

Henry-James shook his head. "Whippoorwill done warned us. Everything gonna be all right, 'cause of you."

Austin blinked at him. Did that mean Seton and Brawley had gotten away? There was no use asking. A slave wasn't always free to tell the truth—like he was.

Austin just closed his eyes as Henry-James left. He didn't open them until he heard a clear voice say, "I'm sorry for what I said last night, Austin."

Charlotte was beside him, her freckles like pepper against her pale skin.

"What's the matter?" Austin said. "You look sick."

"I'm afraid."

"Of what?"

"That you're going to be mad at me forever for yelling at you last night. I was mean to you, and I didn't want to be because so many other people were—Mama and Polly. . . ."

"It doesn't matter. I'm not mad at you," Austin said and swallowed hard. "But you might be mad at *me* again when I tell you what I'm going to do."

Her mouth began to crumple. "You're going to tell, aren't you? You're going to tell my daddy."

"Tell me what, sweet thing?"

"Drayton, what a nice surprise!" Austin's mother said. She held out her arms to her brother, and Uncle Drayton went to her from the doorway.

Ria got up abruptly from her chair and backed toward the door. "I was just nursin' Massa Austin, Marse Drayton," she said. "Miz Kady come to fetch me."

"Then she brought the best," Uncle Drayton said.

"She did indeed," said Mother. "And Drayton, I think Ria could do a great deal of good for me."

Uncle Drayton gave a firm nod. "Then that's the way it shall be," he said. "You'll tend to Miz Sally whenever she needs you," he said to Ria. He squeezed Mother's hands. "I've been neglecting you with all this mess going on. What else can I do for you?"

"You can help my son," she said. "Show him that you are a fair man."

Uncle Drayton looked toward the bed, but his eyes were on Charlotte. "I wondered what we had over here," he said. "Austin, if it has anything to do with the kitchen fire, dismiss that from your mind. Your Aunt Olivia suggested to me that you started it, and I told her that was ridiculous." He cocked an eyebrow. "Was that what you were going to tell me?"

Austin took a deep breath. *Jesus, be my friend,* he thought. *Because if Uncle Drayton says no, I won't have any others.*

"I am friends with Henry-James," he said. "He's the smartest boy I've ever known—besides myself. And last night when I was outside without permission, he helped me get home safe. It's sure he has more sense than I do, and I want to be allowed to be his friend. And while I'm at it, I think it's wrong for you to forbid Charlotte to play with him, because he would never hurt her—or anybody."

Uncle Drayton looked at him long and hard, his brown eyes sharp with the thoughts going through his head. Austin's heart was racing, but there were no more lies in it.

"The first day you came I said you looked like a Ravenal," Uncle Drayton said finally. "But there is a fair share of Ravenal *inside* you, too." His eyes twinkled. "*Sally* Ravenal. I could no more keep you from being friends with someone than my father could her when she was your age. Isn't that right, Ria?"

Ria shivered a little, but she said clearly, "Yes, Marse."

Uncle Drayton leaned his long frame over and patted Austin on the shoulder. "You do as you wish, Austin. I promised your father I would not try to turn you into a Southron."

"And what about Charlotte?"

"Miss Charlotte," he said. His face grew stern. "You've been with Henry-James—against my wishes?"

Charlotte looked at Austin, her eyes filled with tears. Austin nodded to her. *You can do it,* he tried to say with his face. *You've got a friend.*

"Yes, sir," she said.

To Austin's surprise, Uncle Drayton just said, "Why?"

"He's my friend," Charlotte said. "And no one else was . . . until Austin. I was lonely, Daddy!"

"But I must have control over my black folks—especially at this time, with the slaves hearing about the trouble between North and South. I've had one run away already."

"Henry-James is a child, Drayton!" Sally Hutchinson cried. "And so are Charlotte and Austin! Why must they suffer because of a fight we adults have created with our politics?"

Uncle Drayton looked at Charlotte. "Are you suffering, my sweet thing?"

Charlotte nodded.

He pulled her close to him and rested his chin on the top of her head. "All right," he said. "You may have this boy for your friend if you must, as long as he never again shows me disrespect."

"I'll see to that, Marse Drayton," Ria said.

I don't know if anyone can expect that of Henry-James, Austin thought. But the light in Charlotte's eyes made him grin. She wasn't suffering anymore.

"However," Uncle Drayton said, holding Charlotte at arms' length to look at her, "you still disobeyed me."

"Now, Drayton," Mother said.

"I know a good punishment!" Austin said suddenly. "Order her to play with Jefferson all day. That's the worst punishment *I* can think of!"

Uncle Drayton kept the sternness in his mouth, but Austin could see that his eyes were twinkling once again. "You're a cruel taskmaster, Austin," he said. "You go find the little man, Charlotte. And let the drudgery begin."

He kissed her soundly on the cheek and went over to sit beside Mother while Ria hurried from the room.

How could anyone so kind and gentle, Austin thought, *treat his slaves like property?*

He eased back into the pillows and sighed. At least now he was going to have a chance to explore that question. He felt a tugging on his sleeve. Charlotte was grinning at him, her face golden and shining once more.

"What?" he said. "You have to go find Jefferson."

"I know," she whispered. "I love Jefferson!"

"I know," Austin said smugly.

"But I wanted to tell you one more thing. What I said last night, about . . . well, you can call me Lottie, too."

"I will, then," Austin said.

"Do you have a nickname?" she said. "What should I call you?"

Austin cocked his head and thought, and then he gave a satisfied nod. "You can call me just what I am," he said to her. "You can call me Boston Austin."

✝ ✝ ✝